Dear Reader:

As 1981 draws to a close amid holiday bustle and good cheer, the SECOND CHANCE AT LOVE staff wants to thank you, the reader, for making this an exciting year for us. Your enthusiastic letters and strong support have made our venture into romance a tremendous success.

Now, as we look forward to 1982, we are happy to announce the expansion of the SECOND CHANCE AT LOVE line to include six romances each month beginning in January. You will experience the thrill and the torment, the promise and the fulfillment of true love in every one of our special stories each month.

From all of us at Jove to you, best wishes for a wonderful holiday season and a New Year filled with peace, hope and happiness.

Sincerely,

Carolyn Nichols

Carolyn Nichols
SECOND CHANCE AT LOVE
Jove Publications, Inc.
200 Madison Avenue
New York, New York 10016

Second Chance at Love™

DESTINY'S SPELL

SUSANNA
COLLINS

A JOVE BOOK

DESTINY'S SPELL

First Jove edition published December 1981

First printing

"Second Chance at Love" and the butterfly emblem are trademarks be-
longing to Jove Publications, Inc.

Printed in the United States of America

Jove books are published by Jove Publications, Inc.,
200 Madison Avenue, New York, NY 10016

chapter 1

GAZING DOWN FROM the sky, Titania thought Naupaka Island looked like a sparkling emerald surrounded by shimmering necklaces of turquoise and lapis. Once again his face came back to her, the dark blue eyes that seemed to reflect all the whimsical hues of the Hawaiian seas.

As the plane circled around the island, the wing dipped low so that she could see the new construction. It suddenly angered her. Why did they have to change the gracious old hotel?

The pilot was asking them to fasten their seat belts for landing. The momentary anger subsided and was replaced by the mounting thrill of returning to Naupaka. Her heart beat faster as the plane descended. Titania felt like a seventeen-year-old girl again, full of impossible dreams and brilliant expectations.

Feeling generous and giddy, she magnanimously forgave them the new construction. After all, if it weren't for the new shopping arcade, she would not be coming back here. And it wasn't the charming old hotel's fault she held so possessively to her memories of the place. It was the memory of Kimo.

A lifeguard! She laughed at her silly, youthful self. How many fluttering summertime hearts of fawning teenage girls had he captured? And where was he now? Probably selling insurance in Honolulu: a bloated, balding man with a harried wife and three ornery kids; a man who drank beer out of cans while watching football on TV; who bragged to his friends about his amorous conquests as a summer lifeguard in a Hawaiian resort.

But even those sobering, morbid speculations could not dampen the excitement she felt on returning to Naupaka. She would continue to remember the magic of that night as one treasures a favorite fairy tale from childhood. To her, he would always be nineteen, a bronzed, golden-haired god of the sea.

She took a small gold-framed antique mirror from her purse as the plane taxied down the runway. After a quick objective appraisal, she decided to put on more lipstick. Titania wore far less makeup than most women in her business. It would have been superfluous. Her smooth skin already glowed from a soft, flattering California suntan.

Titania Evans had the knack of making everything she wore look as though a top fashion designer had created the look especially for her. Even the long honey-brown hair that she swept off her oval face and clasped back with tortoiseshell combs seemed to be in the latest fashion, though she had been wearing that style for years.

The Cessna taxied to a halt in front of a small building, and, as she began to step off the plane, a masculine hand reached out to help her.

"Mrs. Evans?" Looking up she met the twinkling black eyes of a handsome man who seemed to be a mixture of island races. "I'm Kimo Vasco, the general manager of Naupaka. Mr. Lane is sorry he couldn't come out to meet you personally, but he is tied up with contractors."

When he said the name "Kimo" her heart jumped. A

common Hawaiian name, she reminded herself, and this Kimo looked nothing like the one she remembered so vividly—except in build. The other Kimo had also been tall with broad shoulders.

"I don't know how you manage to look so cool, Mrs. Evans," he said as he picked up her luggage.

The tropical humidity was indeed a shock, even after the brief stopover in Honolulu. "I'm not really cool. Maybe it's the dress that gives you that impression." It was a white, strapless crepe, a stunning dress that had just come in from New York.

"I suppose if anyone would know how to dress for a tropical resort, you would, eh? I feel sorry for these poor tourists from the East Coast in the winter, stepping off the plane in their heavy wool suits."

"Next time you see one, suggest they stop off in Beverly Hills first and visit my store," she said jokingly.

"I don't know," he returned with a teasing glance. "They stop off at your store, maybe they blow all their money and can't afford Naupaka. Better you open your store here."

He helped her into a peach-colored hotel jeep. The airstrip was a few miles from the hotel. Titania took a deep breath, inhaling the fragrance of flowers and sea—that special blend of intoxicating scents that she suspected could exist nowhere else on earth but Naupaka. A flood of happy memories came back to her in a pleasant, tingling rush.

"You sure look familiar, Mrs. Evans. Have you stayed at Naupaka before?"

"A long time ago," she answered vaguely. "Naupaka is every bit as beautiful as I remember—though I could see all the new construction as we flew in."

Kimo sighed and nodded. "Yeah. I kinda miss it the

old way, but that's progress, huh?" He gave her another thoughtful, appraising glance. "How long ago were you here?"

"Oh, let's see, it must have been about twelve years, I guess." There was no guesswork. She could have told him to the day, the hour.

"Wow, then you really will see some changes! Hey, didn't you come here with your grandparents or something?"

She gave a start that he would remember such a detail. "Why, yes. We were only here for a day . . . uh, and a night. You must have an excellent memory for faces."

Kimo broke into a wide grin, showing a set of large, perfectly formed white teeth that sparkled against his dark face. "I was a bellhop then, but I remember you very well. There are still a few of us around from the old days."

The way he said these last words made her uneasy. "Anyone still here I'd remember?" she asked casually, as though it meant nothing.

"Let's see." He rubbed his chin. "Do you remember Kui, who took the catamarans out?"

"No, I don't think so. I never got a chance to take a catamaran ride, we were here such a short time."

"Well, he's still around."

"Still taking catamarans out?"

"Oh, yeah. Let me think who else might have been around. Ralph, the old bookkeeper, is still here, but you wouldn't have known him. He stays in the back office. Still bookkeeping. Now, who else?"

She had the distinct impression he was testing, even teasing her. Was it possible the other Kimo was still there? She straightened her shoulders and took a deep breath. "I do remember a lifeguard . . ."

"Ha! You and about a hundred other wahines!" Kimo

shook his fingers in the air and laughed heartily.

"Wahines?" Her heart was sinking.

"That's Hawaiian for 'girls.' You'd be surprised how many wahines come over here asking what ever happened to the handsome lifeguard."

"Well?" She couldn't meet his eyes for fear he'd detect her turbulent feelings.

"Well what?" Kimo had pulled up in front of the hotel. A doorman was helping Titania out.

"Whatever happened to the lifeguard?" She was certain now he was playing with her.

Kimo's black eyes danced as he grinned. "Yeah, he's still hanging around."

"Still lifeguarding?"

"Nah. You can't go bellhopping and lifeguarding all your life, eh? Come on, let me show you to Mr. Lane's office. What are you drinking? How about a welcome mai tai? I should say a welcome-back mai tai."

It suddenly infuriated her to think that she might have been made the butt of some ribald hotel joke, even though it had all transpired twelve years ago. What right did that rogue of a lifeguard have to tell the entire staff? She fairly shook with humilitation as she seated herself in a white wicker chair on the lanai that served as Acheson Lane's outer office.

It was one thing to speculate about the lifeguard, quite another to be confronted with the glaring reality of his treason. It might have been another amusing moonlight escapade for him, but it had been her private enchanted treasure for twelve years. She resented his treating it so cheaply. With a sudden regret, she was sorry she had returned to Naupaka.

It's what you get for weaving fantasies, Titania, the stern voice of her grandmother echoed in her mind. Unconsciously she patted her briefcase. It was solid and reassuring. Business relationships were built on carefully worded, legal-sized sheets of paper and didn't depend on cloudy wisps of dreams. Her usual composure slowly returned and she was grateful for the few moments to make herself psychologically ready to meet the owner of Naupaka. From what she'd heard, Acheson Lane was a shrewd businessman. She'd need all her wits about her to deal with him.

The office door opened and a tall man in a well-tailored white linen suit stepped onto the lanai. "Mrs. Evans, sorry to keep you waiting. Pleased to meet you. I'm Acheson Lane."

Her lips parted in shock. He was taller, more powerfully built than she had remembered him. There were lines around his mouth and at the corners of his electric blue eyes. But it was the same rugged, tanned face, even though there were beginning flecks of gray in his sun-streaked, golden hair.

No wonder Kimo had been amused.

chapter 2

"*YOU'RE* ACHESON LANE?" She stood up so quickly her vision blurred and she had to hold onto the wicker chair to keep her balance.

Unsmiling, he strode forward to shake her hand in a businesslike manner. She was sure he hadn't recognized her. Of course, he hadn't! What conceit to think he'd remember one—what did Kimo call them?—wahine, when there had been hundreds.

"You seem surprised, Mrs. Evans."

"Oh, it's just that, well, I was here a long time ago. You probably don't remember me. I mean there's no reason you should. But you said your name was Kimo then. I never expected you to be Acheson Lane."

He smiled slightly, but without apology. "I lied."

Two words, so very simply put, but the betrayal held her chest like a vice, crushing it between cruel tongs. She had to stop her mind racing from the present to the past. This is a business trip, she chided herself. It's ludicrous to be hurt twelve years later because of the thoughtless lies of a nineteen-year-old boy who was only out for a little fun.

His deep blue eyes held hers for a long moment in which he seemed to be studying her intensely. "I lied about my name, that is."

7

Her knees felt like jelly and she was grateful for his steady hand on her arm, guiding her into his office. He offered her a chair in front of his dark teakwood desk and went around to the other side. The bay window behind the desk opened onto a breathtaking view of Naupaka Bay.

"I wondered if it was you when I heard your unusual first name, Mrs. Evans," he begun pleasantly.

"Please call me Titania," she corrected him, imitating his friendly, businesslike tone. "Besides, the 'Mrs.' part of my name was extinguished last year."

"You and Jeremy Evans are no longer married?"

"I don't know why people always react with such amazement," she said matter-of-factly. "People get divorced every day."

He raised his eyebrows and leaned back slightly in his chair. A smile played at the edges of his mouth. "You have to admit it's odd for people to dissolve their marriage but leave their business partnership intact."

"Whatever the failings of our marriage, the store continues to flourish. If you have children, you don't abandon them when you get divorced. Jeremy Evans, Ltd. was like our child. We fed and nourished it, raised it up to be the most successful resort-clothing store in Beverly Hills. It would have broken our hearts to turn it over to foster parents."

"It's a shame more divorced parents don't feel that way about their children," he said wryly. "You must have a good relationship with your ex-husband."

"I respect his business sense. We keep our personal feelings away from work. The grave mistake of any man-woman relationship in business is to mix emotion with it, don't you agree?"

He seemed to be concentrating for the moment on something other than what she was saying, though he never lost contact with her eyes. "Yes, of course. Emotions can confuse even the smallest of decisions."

His answer encouraged her to continue. "The store has actually done much better now that Jeremy and I are strictly business partners." There. She had made her point to Acheson Lane, and not too subtly. But he seemed mildly amused. Did he guess that she was desperately building a wall between them for her own protection? This man had already betrayed her once—even though it was over a decade ago. She would take no chances. After Jeremy, Titania was too cautious ever again to play carelessly with matches.

"I have heard wonderful things about your Beverly Hills store. Jeremy Evans, Ltd. is exactly the kind of exclusive shop I want for our new arcade." She breathed easier. He had taken the hint. They were back on an impersonal business level she could deal with.

"Your terms were most attractive." She took a file folder out of her briefcase. "There was only one item, and your lawyer suggested I speak to you about it when I was here."

"I was willing to come down to ten percent, but it would be impossible to go any lower."

"No," she interrupted him, waving her graceful, manicured fingers over the contract, "ten percent is reasonable. It's paragraph eight. About the fixtures."

He took the contract from her and read the paragraph. It stated that the Naupaka Hotel would not provide fixtures for the store. "I didn't think this would be a problem. It's very unusual for a hotel to provide fixtures for a new store."

"It's unusual for a store to be located on such an isolated island," she shot back with firmness.

He shifted his weight in his chair and glanced over at her with amusement. It was a small point, she knew, though it would cost him some money. He could easily concede it. The hotel was crawling with contractors and carpenters. But he shook his head decisively and handed the contract back to her.

She gazed at him steadily, and their eyes locked. She would not back down without a struggle.

"Why don't I show you around the hotel, the new shopping arcade, the new building. You may decide you don't want to open a store here, and all this haggling over a fine point would be for naught." He smiled engagingly at her.

"That's quite true." She tucked the contract back in the file folder. "Actually, Jeremy is not crazy about opening a store here. He's from London and hates the tropics. The only way he'll agree to it is if I come over here personally and run the store."

Acheson leaned forward with interest. "You yourself would be coming over here to live and manage it?"

"At least until I find a competent manager to take over."

He reached over the desk for her file folder and pulled out the contract. Under the paragraph where it stated, "The Naupaka Resort Hotel will not provide fixtures . . ." he crossed out the word "not" and put his initials in the margin.

She flushed deeply when she saw what he'd done. "Mr. Lane." She took a deep breath.

"We're on a first-name basis, remember?" There was a mocking, inviting tone in his voice.

"And that's as intimate as it gets," she added coolly, angered at his audacity in dredging up their past.

"I thought you'd be pleased to get your fixtures," he said.

"The fixtures, yes, but this is everything I loathe in a business relationship. Why is it that a man can't sit down with a woman and treat her on a one-to-one basis without all this sexual innuendo?"

"You're certainly not leaving anything to innuendo," he mused. "You feel that I'm attempting to buy your affections with some store fixtures?"

"Yes."

He shrugged and reached for the contract. "Then we'll change it back. Would that make you feel any better?"

"Not at all. I simply prefer everything aboveboard, no misunderstandings. Sex and business, like oil and water, do not mix. You are a very attractive man," she sermonized, "and I'm sure that..." She paused to find the right words, but they were not forthcoming.

He seemed almost taken off guard by the acid resolution in her voice. She hoped her dark eyes did not betray the vulnerability and turmoil that seethed below the surface.

"You were saying you were sure that..." he repeated, prodding her to continue.

"Well, that night twelve years ago," she began again, horrified that her voice was sounding so unnaturally thin. She wanted to treat their past encounter as a matter of little importance. "We were very young."

"Yes, we were," he agreed, "very young."

With great effort, she composed herself. "I just think it should be understood from the outset that if we are going to do business..." Her face flushed crimson again in spite of her Herculean efforts to prevent it. Behind his desk she could see out the bay window to the curving expanse of white sandy beach and the Pacific Ocean with its many hues of turquoise and blue—so much like Acheson Lane's eyes that gazed steadily at her, waiting for her to continue.

"Titania," he said softly, "the princess."

"You remembered that?" She drew her breath in.

"I've forgotten nothing about that night," he said slowly. "And you?"

chapter 3

TITANIA'S MIND WAS racing back to that enchanted summer of her seventeenth year when she had first come to Naupaka. The mysterious legends of a forbidden island inhabited by elves and upside-down waterfalls had intrigued her as a child, even though she was strictly forbidden by her grandparents to indulge in fairy-tale fantasies. Fantasy had been the undoing of Titania's mother, they reasoned, and they were not going to allow their granddaughter the same mistake.

Although her grandparents traveled constantly, they rarely took Titania out of boarding school to join them unless it was for an educational tour. Those trips were usually dreary, pedantic expeditions during which she was expected to march across miles of museum corridors. But the year she graduated from high school, they made an exception. She could pick her own vacation spot as a graduation present. Without hesitation, she chose the island of Naupaka.

They were surprised she would even remember the old Hawaiian resort where they had stayed many years before on a return trip from the Orient. Titania had been at boarding school at the time and had looked up Naupaka in a children's book on Hawaii, learning about the legends. But her grandparents had been far more impressed

13

by the wealth and exalted social status of the hotel guests, the elegant decor, service, and food, than by the legends.

They had heard the resort was not what it used to be in their day, but the rates were reasonable. And, after all, it was what Titania had chosen. But when they arrived, they were shocked at the deterioration that had taken place in the years since their last visit.

The once-famed Naupaka had become run-down and dirty, the food barely edible, the staff surly and ill-trained. It had taken Titania's grandmother only a few hours to make up her mind to leave, despite Titania's protests. But there was no outbound flight until the following day, and they were forced to spend the night.

Titania was delighted. She loved the gracious old hotel with its wide verandas and didn't mind the peeling paint. The overgrown, untended shrubbery added a sense of mystery to it. The air was thick and fragrant, the scenery spectacular. It was the first real vacation of her life and she was determined to enjoy it.

He had been the golden boy on his lifeguard tower by the pool—lazy blond hair streaked almost white by tropical sun; straight brown eyebrows stretched over startling blue eyes, containing all the glistening shades of the Pacific.

She had watched him stand up on the lifeguard tower, stretch the muscles of his young, broad shoulders like a lion, then make a perfect, effortless dive off the high tower, slicing the water with barely a splash. With long, swift strokes, he swam over to where she lay by the pool.

"How long are you staying here?" He pushed the blond hair from his eyes. Never in her life had she seen a young man as handsome as this lifeguard, and she felt her skin tingle as he smiled at her.

"We're staying just tonight." She could barely speak, her throat was so constricted.

"Just one night?" He didn't try to mask his disappointment. "How come?"

"My grandmother says this place is a real dump and that the Lanes are ugly drunks. It used to be nice, I guess, but they let it get run-down."

Aside from the smile leaving his face, he showed no other outward reaction, so she had no way of knowing how deeply her words must have cut into him. "Will you go out with me tonight?" He wasted no more time.

"I . . . I'd like to, but I don't think my grandparents would let me go out with somebody they didn't know. They're very strict. Maybe if you introduced yourself . . ."

"Probably wouldn't do any good," he said quickly. "Lifeguards have terrible reputations. What time do they go to bed?"

"Oh, very early. Usually before ten." As she said it, she realized he was suggesting that she sneak out to meet him. It was unthinkable. Never in her life had she done anything devious.

Her grandmother was sitting under an umbrella at the other side of the pool reading a magazine, but Titania saw her look up and notice the handsome lifeguard with her granddaughter. It was the elderly woman's opinion that "young men can be too handsome for their own good." She had often pointed out this maxim to Titania, using her own mother as an example of how far astray handsome young men could lead you. Putting the magazine on the table, she strode over to where the young people were talking.

The lifeguard, with his sharp eyes trained to be alert for signs of danger, saw the "threat" come toward them. "Meet me on the beach at midnight," he whispered to Titania before her grandmother was within earshot, "and wear a bathing suit." He then slipped beneath the water like a dolphin, swimming the entire length of the pool underwater.

Settling back into his perch at the top of the tower, he gazed down at her with a mischievous grin.

Since there was no way to tell him she wouldn't meet him without climbing to the top of the lifeguard tower and thereby further arousing her grandmother's suspicions, she found herself caught helplessly in a web of conspiracy without any intention of following through. But that night as her grandparents snored peacefully in the other room, she tossed restlessly in bed, her eyes lighting constantly on the travel clock on her bed stand. As the hour approached midnight, she could no longer restrain herself. She put on her white, two-piece bathing suit and a terry-cloth cover-up. If he had specified a bathing suit, surely he meant to take her swimming, unless . . . She put the thought out of her mind. Of course he meant to take her swimming. A swimming suit was probably what every girl wore on a date in Hawaii.

Despite her beauty, Titania, at seventeen, had not done much dating. It was another vital area in which her grandparents were determined not to fail a second time. She was sent to a strict, all-girls boarding school, and the few boys she met were carefully screened in advance by her grandmother. None of them would have dreamed of suggesting she sneak out for a midnight beach date.

He was standing at the water's edge, arms folded, gazing out into the night. No longer in his white lifeguard uniform, he was wearing loose-fitting, faded Hawaiian print trunks and obviously had been swimming already, for they clung damply to his narrow, well-formed hips. A strong gust of warm wind ruffled his blond hair, which reflected silver in the moonlight.

Sensing her presence, he turned and grinned. "Have any trouble sneaking out?"

It didn't seem to occur to him that she might not have wanted to come. "They were sound asleep." She tried to affect an air of unconcern.

He immediately saw through her. "This the first time you ever snuck out?"

She nodded. He smiled but started to walk without touching her. His long strides were difficult to keep up with and she found herself half skipping, half running to stay alongside him.

"Where're we going?" She tried to appear curious, not worried.

They were at the north end of the beach which ended at some rocks jutting out into the ocean. He took her hand to help her over some precarious spots where the surf rushed in, splashing foam against the black rocks. He seemed to know the path so well he didn't even look down.

"Ever been surfing?" he asked her.

"No, though I've watched surfers in Malibu. Isn't it dangerous to go out there at night?"

"Not if you know the area well, and I've surfed here all my life. You scared?"

"No, of course not," she lied.

"I didn't think you would be. You don't look like the fragile type. I can't stand shrinking violets. Girls in Hawaii all surf and paddle canoes."

She resented his comparing her to the local girls. "I play a lot of tennis," she said quickly, to bring herself up in his esteem.

"Once you've been surfing, there won't be anything else," he said with confidence. "Tennis will be boring."

He produced a surfboard from behind a palm tree. It was the old-fashioned, heavy wooden type, but he lifted it with ease and took it down to the water.

"Why'd we come all the way down here?" she asked him as he pulled a piece of white wax out of his pocket and began rubbing the board with it.

"The waves are better, and on the other beach there

are some rocks in the shallow water you can't see as you're coming in. Now, climb on. I'll show you how to paddle." He demonstrated how she should cup her hands and shove the water back in even strokes. "Good, you've got the hang of it."

"Where's *your* board?" She glanced around.

"This *is* my board. I wouldn't send you out alone. We're going tandem. When we catch a wave, you just lie there and I'll stand up and steer it with my weight. It's easy, you'll see."

She gulped hard as she looked out at the dark ocean, immense and threatening in its vastness—a monster that could easily swallow them up. But she wouldn't for any reason show herself any less brave and daring than the Hawaiian girls he spoke about.

Titania remained frozen as he slid on behind her and began paddling out. "Try to keep in time with me as I tell you: one, two, one, two, that's it."

She obeyed, afraid not to. But the precarious position they were in compounded her guilt at having sneaked away from her grandparents. A picture of the Malibu surfers suddenly flashed through her mind. She had seen them going out in tandem like this before, but it had never struck her as being brazen, and she wondered at the tingling, vulnerable feelings she'd never had before, deep in the lower half of her body.

"Lift up your head, arch your back," he called as they came up on a wave. She was sure it would come crashing down on their heads, but he maneuvered the board so that they went over at an angle, gliding gently over the crest. Having only watched from the beach, she had not imagined the waves to be so high.

"We'll get out just a bit farther and wait for a good set."

They continued to paddle until the lights of the hotel

seemed tinier than the stars above them. But out beyond where the waves were breaking it was quieter. The black dome of the sky seemed less forbidding, and the water rocked them with lullaby gentleness. "I wouldn't mind if we just stayed out here for a while," she said tentatively. "It's so beautiful."

"There's nothing like it in the world," he agreed. "Okay, now get ready. Here comes a set."

She could see the rolling waves approach just as he wheeled the board around and faced the beach. "Paddle with me, like we did before, only harder and faster; then when we've caught the wave, just hold on. I'll be right behind you."

"What if I fall off?"

"Swim toward the beach. I'm not worried about you. You're a good swimmer. I watched you today. And don't forget, I'm a lifeguard. Okay, wahine! Here we go!"

His strong arms were digging into the water more powerfully than before and she kept up with him as best she could as they raced the wave. Then suddenly they were lifting up. He gave another powerful thrust, and they were airborne, riding smoothly in a curl below the white crest. He was standing up behind her, his legs slightly bent, swaying back and forth expertly to keep them balanced. His blond hair whirled around his head and his tan face seemed to be one huge, ecstatic grin. "Like it?" he yelled at her.

"Fantastic!" she shouted back. The salt water sprayed around her, in her mouth, her eyes. The thrill and speed was like nothing she had ever imagined.

"Can we go out again?" she asked him excitedly when the wave had run out and he kneeled back down on the board.

"We can go out all night!" He laughed. They paddled out again and again. Each thrill was greater than the last.

After a few hours, as they reached the place where they waited for the waves he slid off the board. "This time, you solo."

"Oh, I couldn't."

"Just kneel the first time. And if you feel off balance, don't stand up all the way."

"I don't think I could catch a wave all by myself."

"No, your shoulders and arms aren't strong enough. I'll push you into it."

"Hey, I don't know. I'd just as soon you were there."

"Come on, all the girls over here surf. You'll love it."

That did it. She wouldn't let him think she wasn't as good as they were.

This time when the wave came, he shoved the board hard into it. She paddled as she had been taught, using every muscle—then there was the upward movement, the floating. She had caught. Tentatively, she began to raise up, one knee at a time, shifting her weight. The board seemed glued to the wave in perfect balance. Perhaps it wasn't really hard at all.

She stood up on her left foot, then the right, crouching at first; then she let go of the edges of the board and stretched her arms straight out for balance. But she was moving too close to where the wave was breaking, and the sudden force, combined with her own inexperience, caused the board to fly out from under her. Tossed like a toothpick in the powerful breaker, the board missed her by mere inches.

She tried to swim toward shore against the backward motion of the current pulling her out. She was helpless, terrified. Another wave broke over her, shoving her down under the water, throwing her back up, and leaving her gasping for breath.

As she surfaced another time, she saw the lifeguard beside her. "Can you make it?" he yelled over the roar.

As frightened as she was, she was mortified at the thought of him having to haul her in. She put all her strength into the effort and swam with him at an angle toward shore to avoid the undertow.

The board had washed up on the beach, and he went to retrieve it. When he returned to her, he was carrying her terry-cloth top. Shivering, she pulled it gratefully around her shoulders.

"Aren't you cold?" she asked him with surprise.

"When you're out here every night, your skin gets thick."

They remained silent for a few moments, watching the waves. How gentle they looked from shore. "You'd have done all right if you hadn't tried to get up so fast," he told her.

She nodded. "I just felt so secure there for a minute."

"The ocean's like that. One minute you feel secure and the next, it trips you up. Kind of like life," he said philosophically. "What's your name? Funny, we've been together all this time and we don't even know each other's names."

"Titania."

"What kind of a name is that?"

"Titania was the queen of the fairies in Shakespeare's *Midsummer Night's Dream*. My mother was an actress, and she was playing that role when she got pregnant with me."

"That would make you a fairy princess," he said grinning. "Does you mother still act?"

"She passed away several years ago. I didn't know her very well."

"And your father?"

"He gave up acting a long time ago. He and my mother were in the same Shakespeare troupe, but now he runs a drama workshop in Greenwich Village. I've only seen

him a few times in my whole life, and even then my
grandparents weren't too happy about it. Not that it
makes much difference to him. He's never even sent me
a birthday card."

"Yeah, parents are pretty weird," he said as though
he spoke from experience.

"What do your parents do?" she asked him.

"Oh, they work around here," he said absently, "when
they're sober."

They lay back on some grass mats that had been left
there by guests and gazed up at the stars.

"What's your name?"

"Kimo," he answered after a short pause.

"You work here all year round?"

"No, just summers. I come over to lifeguard. I go to
the University of Hawaii."

She was feeling warmer now and let her terry-cloth
top fall open unconsciously as she shifted around on the
mat. They were both propped up on elbows, facing each
other as they talked. But the natural tension that was
bound to exist between two ripe young bodies was mounting. Titania's skin was still tingling from the salt water.
She was lightheaded from the thrill of surfing and even
more lightheaded from the mystery playing in the depths
of the blue eyes of the intriguing young man stretched
out so close to her. There was something tightly coiled
and primitive about him, like the island of Naupaka—
hauntingly beautiful, yet forbidden.

"I like you, Titania," he said huskily. "Too bad you're
only staying the night."

Slowly, he reached out and touched her smooth cheek
and, when she didn't resist, moved closer and placed his
lips on hers.

Titania had been expecting the hard, tight-mouthed
pressure of the boys she knew, but this was different.

His mouth was sensual and warm, brushing her lips at first, moving against them, almost as though he were whispering to her. He caressed her bare shoulder, kissed her slender neck. She lay back on the mat and the taut muscles of his chest pressed against her, taking her breath away. She felt small and helpless with a hundred new sensations pulsing through her veins.

They rolled onto the cool sand, and he pulled her on top of him, wrapping his long legs around hers so that they entwined. His large, strong hands slid up and down her narrow back and, before she could protest, he unhooked her bathing-suit top and threw it just out of reach in the sand.

Embarrassed and ashamed, she covered her bare breasts. Gently but firmly he removed her hands, pinning them at her sides. "You're beautiful, Titania," he said, looking at her breasts and then into her eyes. "Don't be afraid. You should be proud of your beauty."

She was too horrified to speak, wondering what he was going to do next.

"You don't want me to touch them?"

She shook her head.

"All right, I won't—if you don't want it. But we can kiss some more. I've never understood why guys can go without tops and not girls." He pulled her gently to him, and she didn't resist. It was a long warm kiss, but his hands, this time, did not move on her. Slowly, she began to relax again, and a new feeling washed over her as her bare breasts rubbed against his hard chest.

Caught up in the breathless wonderment of each other, they soon forgot what he had promised. His hands swept down her back, up her sides, pressing in at her tiny waist. A wild, untamed Titania that she hardly recognized moved feverishly against him. She was a creature that belonged only to him and the island of Naupaka. Having emerged with him from the sea, the very rhythm of the pounding waves crashed within their souls. His strong fingers found her nipples as she arched her back. As his lips plunged down on them, she felt the volcanic fires spring from between her legs. She wanted to cry out for him to stop. Her island being begged her to prolong the sweet agony, surrender herself to his fiery caress.

But seventeen years of rigid morality does not relinquish its hold in a moment. Guilt soon washed over her and drowned out every other sensation. She scrambled up and grabbed her bathing-suit top. With her back turned to him, her hands shaking, she clasped it on as though it were a shield.

He continued to lay there, his mouth slightly open, a lion whose prey had just been snatched from his claws. "How old are you, fairy princess?"

"Seventeen."

"Girls here are much more experienced by your age."

"Good for them," she said harshly, unwilling to take that bait again.

He smiled and put his hands behind his head. "You angry at me or angry at yourself, princess?"

It took the wind out of her sails. "Both, I guess."

"Come sit back here. Come on, it's all over. We'll just talk."

Reluctantly, she sat down a little distance away from him in the sand. She was still trembling.

"You liked it, didn't you?" His voice was husky, but he made no move toward her.

She nodded, looking away from the knowing blue eyes that reflected moonlight.

He sat up on his haunches and looked out to sea, his nostrils dilating as he filled his lungs with the heavy tropical air. The way his silvery blond hair blew around his face, his chin lifted to the moon, he seemed like a young Poseidon, ready to disappear into the sea, a dark realm all his own. "Come on, princess." He took her hand and helped her up. "Better get back to the bungalow before you turn into a pumpkin on me."

They walked to the edge of the water where the sand was damp and hard under their feet. The gentle foam lapped around their ankles. "You're a beautiful enchantress, Titania." He was gazing at her with longing, though he did not touch her. "Pele is in your soul."

"Pele?"

"Goddess of volcanoes, fire, and passion." She wanted to fling herself into his strong arms and feel the warmth of him again, but she stood there silently, unable to speak or act. "There is something about us, princess. It's not usual at all. It's . . . well, I can't explain it."

"Please try," she begged him softly.

"Look, I don't want to sound like I'm bragging, but I don't know how else to tell you. I've had girls— women. Well, here in the islands it's different. Life is looser than on the mainland, and in a hotel, people on vacation . . . but that's not the point. What I'm trying to say is that you and I have something I've never experienced before. It's like it's a bubbling primitive force that's so intense . . . that's why I thought of Pele but, oh hell!" He kicked the water with powerful force and sent a huge spray of white water back out into the sea. "You're leaving tomorrow."

At the edge of the path that led back to the bungalow, he lifted a strand of her long silky hair, twisting it between his fingers. The sea behind him was turning blue gray with the dawn; and his eyes, blue gray with a regret she was just beginning to understand, were on her.

"If you stayed here I'd take you surfing every night. We'd ride horses up to the Menehune Caves in the rain forests where mountain orchids and ginger blossoms grow wild. I'd take you in an outrigger canoe to beaches nobody knows." His voice trailed off. He plucked a snow-white gardenia from a nearby bush and placed it tenderly over her ear. "And I'd cover your hair with flowers—a crown for my fairy princess." He leaned over and kissed her lightly on the lips, then turned back down to the beach.

Titania watched him for a moment, the tan skin of his strong back turning golden as the red sun appeared over the steep green cliffs. As though to escape from the blinding light of day, he dove into a crashing wave.

Perhaps he was a god who only emerged out of the black sea at night to seduce fairy princesses, she thought, aching to return with him to the sapphire and emerald kingdom. They'd live in castles of coral where she, draped in glistening green necklaces of seaweed, would swim with a train of dolphins and into the strong arms of her golden sea god. Together they would skim across the white crests of curling waves.

Instead, Titania crept back into the bungalow and went to bed, and as the plane circled over the island of Naupaka the next morning, she wondered if she hadn't dreamed it all.

Days, even weeks and months later, she toyed with the idea of sending a postcard to "Kimo the lifeguard" at Naupaka, but when she asked the Hawaiian Tourist Bureau for the address, she was informed that the Lanes had died and the resort had closed down. Naupaka was being used only to raise sugar, pineapple, and cattle.

Though he had called her his princess and swore he had never felt that way about any girl before, he had never once suggested they do something as mundane as correspond. Couldn't he have gotten *her* address from the hotel register?

She quietly tucked the dream and doubts away in a

quiet recess of her mind and secretly thanked her grandparents for discouraging silly flights of the imagination.
Real life was far too harsh to allow for the intrusion of
such fanciful myths.

chapter 4

As ACHESON PROPELLED her through the lobby, Titania began to take note of the changes since she had last been there. Though obviously redecorated, the Naupaka had not bowed to plastic Hollywood decor. There was a light airiness in the white wicker furniture. The cushions were a stunning pattern of pale peach and green Hawaiian floral, while the carpets and paintings subtly echoed the colors.

It was a carefully planned elegance. Not so minor a thing as a vase of flowers was placed haphazardly. The colors of the flowers were also chosen to complement the decor.

"You've done a beautiful job here," she said with admiration. "I'm glad you didn't change the old hotel. There's something so gracious about the white wood and wicker, the wide verandas."

"Most of what I did here will never be seen," he mused. "New wiring, plumbing, kitchen facilities. The decorating was the easy part. I simply hired a decorator."

"But you were smart to find one who understood the old hotel. Some idiot could have marched in here and ruined it." She suddenly noticed that the waiters, moving quietly through the lobby with drinks for guests, had color-coordinated uniforms of pale peach shirts and white pants. "Your decorator didn't overlook a single detail, even your waiters match the lobby!"

"I saw the work this man did on a home in Beverly Hills that was built about the same time as Naupaka, and he'd done an excellent job of updating it without throwing away its soul. By the way, the owner of that home is a customer of yours, Karin Baldwin."

"Ah, yes," sighed Titania. "The beautiful Baldwin."

"You sound as though you're not crazy about her."

"Purely personal reasons. It's hard not to be crazy about a woman who drops six thousand dollars in your store every time she crosses the threshold," Titania answered with a rueful smile.

"Six thousand dollars? No wonder she's always wearing something different." He laughed. "Six thousand dollars buys a lot of clothes."

"Not at Jeremy Evans, Ltd.," joked Titania. "Our jeans run three hundred dollars a pair."

"A measly pair of jeans? You can have a whole room at Naupaka for three hundred dollars a night," he mused. "I'd better revise my rates. These people will think they're getting a bargain. Funny business we're in," he added thoughtfully, "catering to the rich. I bet you'd never spend three hundred dollars on a pair of jeans for yourself."

"It's insane!" she agreed. "I wouldn't spend thirty dollars on a pair of jeans."

Acheson smiled. "And if I'm going on a vacation, I'd just as soon take a backpack and hike out in the open somewhere. I'd never spend three hundred dollars a night on a room."

They stepped across the veranda and down the main stairs into the gardens. "I've never quite figured out why people pay our outrageous prices," Titania admitted. "Do you suppose it's like Mrs. Baldwin—too much money and nothing much to do with her time?"

"What they're buying from people like us is prestige," he said. "You've managed to create an exclusive aura around the name Jeremy Evans, Ltd., and I've done the same thing with Naupaka. It means something to a Karin Baldwin to say she buys her jeans at Jeremy Evans, Ltd. and spends two weeks out of every month at Naupaka. The price tag is understood."

"I don't think prestige is the only reason she comes to Naupaka." Titania gazed up at him slyly.

He gave her a hard, fleeting glance that told her he wasn't interested in pursuing the subject.

"She's a very beautiful woman," continued Titania, choosing to ignore his meaningful silence. She was suddenly curious to see how much Acheson Lane would admit.

"Very beautiful," he agreed. "Of course—it's probably all in the beautiful clothes she wears." He shot her a wry smile.

"I wonder what her poor husband would think if he knew who she was trying to impress with all those clothes." Titania was hoping to see Acheson flinch, but she was disappointed by his composure.

"Mr. Baldwin doesn't leave the Baldwin Bank of Beverly Hills long enough to worry about his wife's wardrobe bills," said Acheson.

"Or her *hotel* bills." Titania asked provokingly, "Does she ever bring him over here with her?"

"Once in a while. He plays a mean game of golf for a man pushing eighty."

"Remarkable." She realized that she was going to get nothing out of Acheson and had just decided to let the subject drop when he stopped under a Plumeria tree and gazed at her. "You're curious to know, aren't you?" A smile played at the edge of his lips.

"About what?" She looked up at him innocently.

"About me and Karin Baldwin."

"Your private life is none of my business, though I'll admit to having an unnatural craving for gossip. It's one of those nasty habits I can't seem to shake no matter how many New Year's resolutions I make."

"I've heard it's easier to give up smoking than gossip. Have you tried hypnosis?"

"Has no effect on gossip, I'm told. And working where I do doesn't help. There's probably more juicy tidbits floating around the Jeremy Evans' dressing rooms than in the offices of the *National Enquirer*." She sighed. "Ever since you reopened Naupaka, a lot of that gossip has revolved around the inimitable Acheson Lane. How could I help being curious?"

Mrs. Baldwin was a gossip lover's dream. The Beverly Hills socialite still looked as beautiful at forty as she had at twenty when she charmed a sixty-year-old widower, owner of one of the largest banks in California, into marrying her. But Karin Baldwin was cut out to be a general, not a wife. She gloried in conquests, and, as she grew older, they became even more important to uplift her only slightly sagging ego. Jeremy Evans had been one of the conquests and Titania one of the casualties.

Acheson took her arm to help her across the dirt path to the new construction site. "You've piqued my interest, dear lady. What in the world is said about the 'inimitable Acheson Lane'?"

She was not about to repeat the volumes of anatomical details she had heard from more women than Karin Baldwin. "I wouldn't want to embarrass you, but suffice it to say that Jeremy Evans, Ltd. was considering sending you a plaque to show our appreciation for your helping us sell so many clothes."

"*I* help you sell clothes?" He looked genuinely surprised, but secretly Titania sensed he was delighted with their playful repartee. It was a side of her Acheson might not have expected from the stiff way she treated the romantic innuendos in his office. She could have fun as long as she wasn't the subject or object of discussion. Once she had established their relationship on a solid base of friendship, she could relax. She wondered if he understood the apparent contradiction.

"The women who come to Naupaka seem determined to bankrupt their husbands in the effort to outdo one another in outfits to woo the handsome owner," she said. "Or haven't you noticed them tripping over each other to get to you as they step off the plane?"

He threw back his head and laughed. "There have been studies done on how too much gossip can affect your perception of reality. Spend a few days here, and I think you'll get a clearer picture of where I spend my time."

"Where's that?"

"Right here."

They were walking toward the new five-story building that seemed to be near completion. "This is the new baby," he told her.

"It's a handsome child!" she noted with admiration.

"There's always the temptation to build something cheap, like the ugly high-rise boxes they've put up all over Waikiki, but I didn't want to lose the feeling of the original Naupaka."

The new building was as close as possible in style to the old without being an exact replica. The private balconies off each room seemed to be more like old-fashioned verandas.

"The new villas are going in over here. Everyone told me I was nuts to go to all that expense in this day and age, but I've always liked the privacy of them, the mystery that surrounds the people who inhabit them."

"Oh, yes," she said enthusiastically, "like the stories of Gable and Lombard secretly meeting in the bungalows of the Beverly Hills Hotel. There's something very romantic about them..." She stopped abruptly, slanting a glance at him through her thick lashes. "Please forgive me. That's my gossip addiction acting up again."

"You're forgiven. Have you ever been able to kick the habit for any length of time?" He feigned the concern of a doctor.

"Four whole days once, but I went through terrible withdrawal."

They both chuckled, moving in unison toward the one villa which was finished. Titania could see how luxurious the villas would be, each with its own swimming pool. "Oh, no, are you really going to have a hot-tub spa right outside the bedroom?"

"You don't think it's a good idea? I thought you liked romance." He had a mischievous look in his blue eyes.

"This isn't romance." She laughed. "This is positively decadent."

Circling around the villas they came to the shopping arcade which was near completion. In fact, a beauty salon was already operating. "There won't be a large profit for you until the new construction is finished," he said, "but the business from the old hotel will be adequate for the time being."

"When is the projected completion date?"

"We're shooting for June for the big building to get the summer traffic and a few months after that for the villas. I also have an open-air nightclub that will be in a separate site down by the beach—dancing under the stars, jazz, and Hawaiian entertainment, and though I loathe it, some disco."

"All you need are rides and you'll have a regular Disneyland," she teased.

"Disney would have killed to have an entire island like this to play with!" He laughed. "I have made accommodations for children, though. I've hired a full-time activity director to arrange horseback riding, outrigger canoe rides, surfing lessons."

"Wholesome entertainment for the kiddies while their parents wallow in the hot tubs." Titania smiled broadly. "Is there *anything* you haven't thought of?"

"No," he said without hesitation. Acheson Lane was not a man of false humility. "Now, the entrance to your store will be here, but being on the corner, you'll have all this window space."

"Whoa! Wait a minute." She stopped him. "I still haven't decided whether I'm going to open a store here."

"Well, if you do . . ."—he held her arm as she stepped gingerly over some two-by-fours left by the construction crew—"the dressing rooms will be back here."

"These aren't dressing rooms, they're cubbyholes. This is a terrible floor plan, if you don't mind my saying so."

"There, you've found something I haven't thought of." His blue eyes twinkled. "I know nothing about women's dress shops. But tell you what, if you decide to open here, I'll construct it any way you like. Fixtures and all. You can have a dressing room the size of the grand ballroom at the Ritz if you want."

"That's very generous." She smiled up at him. "But just a few more square feet would be sufficient. These women are used to having clothes brought in to them. Rarely do they chose anything off a rack. In Beverly Hills, we located next to a good, small restaurant so we could have lunch brought in to the customers. Would I be able to use your room service?"

"Sandwiches, filet steaks, strawberry daiquiris, Boston cream pies—anything you want."

"Strawberry daiquiries?"

"Ramos fizzes, mai tais . . ."

"You're making me thirsty." The humidity and heat were beginning to affect her.

"Where are my manners? I've been rushing you around without so much as a drink. Why don't you take a swim, enjoy a mai tai or a strawberry daiquiri, and we'll meet later on to talk?"

He took her up to the front desk. "Would you prefer a room in the main building or one of the newly remodeled bungalows off the beach?"

She smiled. "For free I shouldn't be fussy." Acheson Lane had mailed her the first-class airline tickets and made it understood on the phone that she was to be his guest at the hotel.

"It's allowed," he said with a grin.

"The bungalow, then," she said impulsively. "It would be lovely to be near the water. When I was here with my grandparents, we had . . ."

"Number twelve," he interrupted her. "I told you, I've forgotten nothing." His eyes seemed to turn a darker shade of blue and she felt an unexpected flutter in her chest in spite of her resolve to keep their relationship friendly but businesslike.

"That bungalow is available tonight." He changed back to a cool tone and took the key from the mailbox. "Paul," he told the reservation clerk, "have one of the bellboys bring Mrs. Evans's luggage to number twelve and have a mai tai sent there, too."

"Oh, Mrs. Evans," said Paul, "your husband called a little while ago. He said he'd try again in half an hour and if he didn't reach you, you were to call him at the store."

She started to correct the misconception that she and Jeremy were still married, but it would have been awkward, as it always was. Just too, too much explanation was required.

Acheson took the key from Paul. "I'll see Mrs. Evans to her bungalow." They walked out onto the veranda, down the stairs, and onto the garden path that led to the beach.

It was a strange sensation, almost a feeling of déjà vu, to be walking with Acheson down the same garden path that had taken her to the moonlit beach so many years ago.

"The gardens are lovely here," she said, to make conversation.

"There wasn't much replanting to be done. My grandmother supervised all the landscaping when the place was built and everything was still growing well, as it inevitably does in the tropics, but these paths were like jungles. It took us months to get them cleared away again."

Titania admired them but was secretly disappointed in the carefully manicured appearance of the gardens now. She had loved the wild untended look, the tall ferns and drooping flowers. "It's so tame now," she said so softly that Acheson may not have heard. Certainly he appeared not to have, for he made no comment.

He unlocked the door for her. "If there's anything you need, let me or my general manager, Kimo Vasco, know. You're welcome to stay here as long as you'd like."

"No," she said quickly, "that would be an imposition on you. I'm here to discuss business—though heaven knows I could use a vacation."

"You have pressing business to get back to?" He placed the key on a white wicker writing table near the window.

"Market week starts Saturday," she lied. It was not until the following week. "I do all the buying for the store. I'll have to return to Los Angeles tomorrow."

"Well, as long as you're here, relax and look around. Get a feel for the place, talk to the people by the pool. I can't expect you to make a decision on the basis of what you've seen so far. How about meeting me on the veranda at five for cocktails? We'll have some dinner and . . ." He paused. "I was going to say take a walk on the beach, but I don't mean it the way . . ."

"We're grown-ups now. A nice walk on the beach might do wonders to clear our cluttered brains," she said briskly, refusing to allow him to see her agitation.

"At five, then." He smiled professionally and strode out the door.

Titania stood at the window watching him walk back toward the hotel. Even in his distinguished white linen suit, the broad shoulders and narrow hips were still those of a young lifeguard, though the cocky swagger of youth had given way to the purposeful step of the grown man.

Did he still talk about the goddess Pele and the Menehune Caves? Did he give gifts of gardenia blossoms? She couldn't help but wonder if he had ever taken Karin Baldwin surfing by moonlight. Karin Baldwin? She laughed out loud. Karin would be terrified to surf—not at the danger, but that she'd muss her hair. No, Acheson seemed to have grown out of all those silly dreams, just as she had. He was no longer a swaggering lifeguard and she was no longer an innocent adolescent.

But there was still something magic in being with him—that feeling of being inside the pulsing heart of a volcano. How was it possible she could feel so attracted to him, it suddenly occurred to her with a shock, when she was still so hopelessly and miserably in love with Jeremy?

chapter 5

SHE STARTED TO pick up the phone to call Jeremy, then decided against it. She had just spoken to him that morning before she left. Whatever he had to discuss with her could wait.

Her luggage arrived simultaneously with a mai tai, a delicious tropical rum drink garnished with a spear of fresh pineapple and a sprig of mint. She took a sip and unpacked her bathing suit.

The one piece suits were cut high at the thigh this year, disastrous for anyone with chubby legs. Titania had some trouble selling them for that reason. With her long slender legs, she looked better in the suit than many of the models who showed them in the fashion magazines.

Tucking her long hair up under a floppy sun hat, the same shade of fuchsia as the suit, she started out the door, but the ringing of the phone brought her back.

"Hi, luv," said the voice on the other end of the line. It was Jeremy. All the turbulent feelings she'd been experiencing with Acheson now turned to guilt. She saw them as a betrayal of her love for Jeremy. Would she ever get used to calling him an *ex*-husband?

"Don't you think it's time you dropped the 'luv'?" she asked with annoyance. He didn't love her; calling her 'luv' was hypocritical.

"It's just the bloody British in me. Can't seem to shake it. How about 'Hello, duckie'?

"Just plain hello would suffice."

"Don't get bitchy, old girl. How's it going in paradise?"

"I saw the arcade. Acheson Lane is doing a first-class job here. Looks good, but I'm going to scout around a little this afternoon. From what I've seen, our clothes are already on half the women here."

"Then what's the use of our clothing them over there? If we're going to put up with the blasted heat, let's open up in Palm Springs where we can at least keep an eye on the store. I can't see traipsing across the Pacific Ocean several times a year."

"We'll be the only women's store in here, Jeremy. It can't miss."

"Well I'll trust your judgment. I always have. But it seems to me he's got a good deal more to gain from having Jeremy Evans, Ltd. in his damn resort than we have from being there."

"That's why the terms of the lease are so good. He's already conceded to putting in fixtures—whatever we want. There are going to be a lot of people coming here, a lot of very wealthy people. I don't think there's any way we can lose money on the deal." She wondered why she was doing such a selling job on Jeremy when she had been so lukewarm to Acheson.

"Unless this Naupaka bombs out big. Hawaiian resorts are a dime a dozen. Air fares are going up. And this place is the most remote of all the islands. There's no guarantee people will go there when they can get the same thing in Honolulu where there are all kinds of stores and restaurants and nightclubs. Why would anyone want to go to such an isolated place? And if it goes under, we go under with it. It's going to be a big investment for us."

"Well, I haven't decided yet," she hedged. "By the way do you know who recommended us to the owner?"

"Karin Baldwin," he replied without hesitation. "She told me. Of course, it's for very selfish reasons she wants us in there. You know how much clothes mean to her. She wants to be sure to have a good source close by so she can continue to impress that owner."

Titania could never quite understand the relationship between Jeremy and Karin Baldwin. It was so casual an affair that they discussed their other lovers openly. It was the kind of relationship Jeremy had wanted to make of their marriage, one of those so-called open marriages. They couldn't come to any agreement on the subject and, finally, angrily, Titania had served him with divorce papers. Intellectually she understood that kind of marriage and did not condemn it. She heard far too many things in her store to be shocked by extramarital affairs. But when all the modern philosophical and psychological rhetoric was cleared away, the inalterable fact remained—she loved Jeremy far too much to bear the thought of his having another woman. Divorce had not made it any easier, as she had hoped it would. A kind of impotent rage sprang to her chest whenever she heard Jeremy mention Karin or any of his other women.

"This Acheson Lane as good looking as they say?" asked Jeremy.

"Better," she said abruptly. For some reason the thought of Acheson Lane, his tanned face and blue eyes, disturbed her more at that moment than Karin Baldwin's name on Jeremy's lips.

"Maybe you ought to indulge in a little..."

"Jeremy, if I want your advice," she said bitingly, "I'll ask for it, *duckie*."

"Don't get your pretty feathers ruffled." He laughed. "And don't get so involved with him you can't make a decent decision about the store."

Titania was irritated by his insinuation. "My emotional state has no affect on my business judgment. You should know that by now."

"I trust you," he assured her. "I was just joking. And hurry back. I miss you."

"Sure, Jer," she said flatly, though the softness in his voice still cut through to a vulnerable place in her heart. She had not really wanted a divorce. Serving him with the papers has been more a plea for him to give up the other women. Never had she expected him to accept it so eagerly, and she still burned with hurt and humiliation that he hadn't bothered to put up even a meager protest. In the back of her mind she knew that she was not hanging onto the store for business reasons as she'd told Acheson. What she desperately hoped was that Jeremy would see the error of his ways and want her back in a traditional marriage. So far it hadn't happened. He went out almost every night, reveling in his new freedom while she sulked alone.

When Acheson Lane's attorney had contacted them about opening a branch in Naupaka, she had jumped at the chance. Since it was proving futile to wait for Jeremy to change, perhaps it would be better to go away for a while, recapture a little of the magic of her youthful dreams at a place like Naupaka. Absence might make all the difference. Jeremy might call saying he missed her, begging her to come back.

What she had not forseen and what now set all her plans awry was the reappearance of "the lifeguard" and his still-powerful, mysterious effect on her.

She wondered if that wasn't the real reason she had returned to Naupaka. Could it be that lurking in the back of her subconscious was the desperate hope that he'd still be here somehow — waiting for her return?

chapter 6

TITANIA WALKED DOWN to the beach. It felt good to
spread her bare toes in the sand. Walking close to the
water, she could look up and study the layout of the
Naupaka Resort with all its new construction. The sparkling old white hotel, whose style betrayed the New
England ancestry of those who had built it, had a gracious
veranda that stretched entirely around the ground floor.

To the left was the original swimming pool nestled
in colorful gardens of tropical flowers. To the right of
that, a sloping lawn dropped down from the veranda of
the hotel to give a spectacular unobstructed view of the
bay. More gardens and bungalows were farther to the
right, each with their private paths leading to the beach.
Then, following the shoreline, was the eighteen-hole golf
course.

The shopping arcade connected the old and new buildings that were so remarkably alike in style. There was
another large swimming pool and tennis courts. The new
villas were built along the golf course, not the beach,
and on an incline high enough to have a spectacular view
of the Pacific Ocean.

She had seen the artists' renderings Acheson had sent,
but standing there, looking up at it all, was quite another
thing: the gracious white buildings set against the verdant

mountain that rose majestically into the clouds, the fragrant gardens that circled like silk ribbons everywhere, the air heavy with the tang of the sea and warm with trade winds. She turned and gazed out at the ocean, resplendent with every shade of blue from turquoise to cobalt. Titania had seen color swatches from designers that were not as complete. She would have to buy special clothes for this place if she decided to stay. Ordinary resort lines would not be adequate. The clothes would have to be vivid and elegant, comfortable and yet unique.

She walked back up to the swimming pool. It had changed little since she had been there last but, like everything that bore Acheson's personal touch, it had been improved. The harsh cement that usually surrounds swimming pools had been replaced by a soft emerald carpet of grass. Along with the pale peach-colored umbrellas, the area was shaded by graceful palm trees that helped cool the sunbathers when the fronds blew in the trade winds. The poolside furniture was expensive wrought iron with patterns of flowers painted white, their cushions plush in pale green and peach fabric. Thick, fluffy beach towels in those colors were supplied by the pool staff who seemed eager to provide every comfort for the guests.

The furniture had not been arranged by chance or in impersonal long rows as in some hotels. It was grouped into conversational areas around tables and lush planters of flowers as though in someone's private home. Larger groupings were for the more sociable of the Naupaka clientele, but small, intimate areas lay hidden amid the ferns and tropical flowers.

The waiters, never obtrusive, were nonetheless in such abundance that Titania began to think one had only to look thirsty for them to appear. Fresh pineapples cut whole with the slices left inside were provided with the tropical rum and fruit drinks.

"I'm so pampered here," one of her Beverly Hills customers confided dreamily. "This is the third time I've been back this year."

"You don't get bored with the same scenery all the time?" asked Titania with surprise.

"Who could tire of this scenery?" She gestured out to the ocean. "Besides, there is no other resort that gives you this kind of service. The first time I arrived, I told the bartender by the pool that I drink only Martini & Rossi sweet vermouth poured over ice cubes made from Perrier water. Habit I got into in Paris. I know it's most annoying to bartenders, but he always remembers and seems so happy to fix it the way I want with just a twist of lemon, like so." She showed Titania the intricate twist of the lemon. "Now, Mrs. Evans, I have traveled all over the world and stayed with some of the most gracious hostesses on three continents, but there is nothing quite like Naupaka for making you feel at home."

"I must say I'm impressed," Titania agreed.

"Oh, how silly, my dear." She laughed. "But that's the way I feel when I go into Jeremy Evans, Ltd. You and the saleswomen always know my name, my dress size, the colors, styles, and designers I prefer."

"But I've never had Perrier ice cubes for your drinks," said Titania. "Believe me, I will from now on." She tried to take note of the way the lemon was twisted. It was a matter of pride. She couldn't let Naupaka outdo Jeremy Evans, Ltd.

"Well, you see my point then," said the woman, smiling. "Of course, one pays dearly for this kind of service. But after all, my own servants are not nearly as attentive as Naupaka's."

Titania also learned that Acheson Lane paid his staff so well that there was a waiting list to work there. At those salaries, he could be choosy and hire only the best. The guests were people who couldn't be bothered with the dirty little business of small change, and Acheson, understanding this, made their lives easier by not bothering them with the inconvenience of paying for their meals or drinks. After all, it was the only place to eat or drink on the island, so at Naupaka, *everything* was included in the daily rate, even tips.

It did not take Titania long to become weary of the inane conversations of these pleasant but generally vapid women, especially when they hadn't a shred of new gossip to hold her interest. Besides, she had not taken a vacation from work in over three years and decided that at least for the few hours left of sunlight, she was going to relax and enjoy this unusual resort. She slipped off to one of the more secluded areas and lay back on the chaise, letting the warm tropical afternoon sun caress her skin. But just as she drifted off into a state of semi-isleep, a shadow hovered over her eyelids. Thinking it was a waiter, she murmured, "No, thanks, I'm not quite ready for another drink."

When the shadow did not disappear as quickly as the waiters did, she blinked her eyes open and saw Acheson Lane smiling at her. "Enjoying yourself?"

Something about his masculine presence made her swing her legs around and sit up instead of lying stretched out vulnerably before him. He took a chair nearby and a waiter magically appeared. "Just a coke for me, Bill, and Mrs. Evans is not quite ready for another drink."

"I just changed my mind." She eyed her evaporated mai tai.

The waiter nodded and zipped off along the narrow path through the ferns.

Acheson was still in a white suit, but his shirt was now a blue pinstripe that caught the color of his eyes.

"Perrier ice cubes?" She smiled up at him.

"Mrs. Galton of Beverly Hills," he answered.

"How do you keep details like that straight—index cards?"

"If you promise not to reveal my secret," he pulled his chair closer, "I'll tell you."

"By all means. I have no memory for dress sizes, and barely one for names even though it's so important in a business like mine. I use index cards."

"I use," he glanced secretly around and then whispered in her ear, "a computer."

"You're putting me on." She laughed. The teasing whisper so close to her face had set her pulse racing.

"Most of the major hotels use them now. We also know if Mrs. Galton likes two blankets and the air conditioner on high; if she prefers a room decorated in shades of gold rather than blue; if she likes gardenias." He plucked one off a neighboring bush and handed it gallantly to Titania. "We leave a gardenia on her pillow every night."

She suddenly remembered the gardenia he had put in her hair many years before.

"Is there any service you *don't* provide?" She could not help but think of all the women who had bragged about having Acheson Lane, not gardenias, on their pillows.

He threw back his golden head and laughed heartily. "There are some things that don't go into the computer."

The waiter arrived with the drinks, then disappeared back into the tunnel of foliage. She took a long sip of the delicious rum drink. "I can't imagine actually being able to *work* in this atmosphere," she sighed. "There you are, all starched in your white suit. Wouldn't you like to be able to sit out here by the pool, too, and sip mai tais?"

Just then an obese woman wearing a turban over her bleached hair with an equally obese little boy waddled up to them. "Mr. Lane, we were wondering if we could take the sunset catamaran ride tonight. Is it too late for reservations? Jason read all about catamarans in school, and ever since we arrived he's been pestering us."

Acheson stood up politely. "Mrs. Rostand, this is Mrs. Evans." By the time Titania finished the "how do you do," a waiter materialized again beside them.

"Aka," he said to the waiter, "Mr. and Mrs. Rostand and their boy would like to go on the sunset catamaran ride tonight. Would you tell Kui to put them on the list?" The waiter hurried off immediately and Acheson turned back pleasantly to the beaming woman. "Is there anything else I can do for you? Jason, would you like to learn how to paddle an outrigger canoe?"

Titania was impressed by the smooth way he handled the guests, treating them as though they were visiting nobility and it was his personal obligation to see that their stay was nothing less than perfect.

"This is the loveliest vacation we have ever had, Mr. Lane," gushed Mrs. Rostand. "I already had my husband make reservations for Christmas vacation and Easter."

"We'll be delighted to see you again!" Acheson said. "And how pleasant it will be for you to get away from New York in the middle of winter."

"Oh, you remembered we were from New York." She giggled. "Come on, Jason. We're going to meet papa on the golf course."

Titania gave him a knowing look. "There's a computer clicking away in your brain."

He looked up at the sky and then squinted out to sea. For a brief second something in the strong line of his jaw, the tension in his muscles, visible even beneath the white suit, the way the breeze ruffled his thick blond hair, reminded her of the lithe young sea god she had once known. He turned smiling eyes back to her. "I shall order a spectacular Naupaka sunset for your entertainment tonight. Would you like that?"

She pretended to consider it. "I do prefer my spectacular sunsets in shades of red and orange with puffy little pink clouds—no thunder and lightning, please."

"One red and orange sunset, hold the lightning," he told a passing waiter who gazed at him with confusion, then continued on down the path.

"Will he put that into the computer?" She suppressed a smile.

"Yes, and every day you are at Naupaka I shall see that you have a spectacular sunset made to order." She had to admit he seemed capable of it.

"But if I find even so much as one Perrier ice cube in my room, I'm going back to Honolulu," she warned.

The confused waiter suddenly reappeared. "Excuse me, Mr. Lane, but about the red and orange sunset you ordered. The bartender wants to know if that's like a navy grog."

"Yes, exactly," said Acheson seriously, while Titania tried not to giggle.

The waiter looked relieved, then added, "And I'm sorry, sir, but what does 'hold the lightning' mean? No pineapple spears?"

"No Perrier ice cubes," Acheson corrected him.

As soon as he left, Acheson and Titania doubled over with laughter. She could not remember when she had laughed so hard.

"See you on the terrace later," he said as he rose to go, "and be careful of that red and orange sunset. It will knock you for a loop."

Titania waited until the last ray of direct sunlight left the pool area, then went back to her bungalow to change for dinner. Because she was already tan from living in

Southern California, she was only lightly sunburned, and it added a beautiful blush to her cheeks.

She smoothed out her new long, deep purple Saint Laurent dress. It was a strapless silk with a slit up the side. She knew from the conversation in her fitting rooms that women dressed elegantly for dinner at Naupaka, and though she preferred informality, looking chic was part of her business. Her own stylishness made clients confident of her judgment. She knew it was the same reason Acheson Lane persisted in wearing a suit and tie despite the heat. He set the tone for Naupaka just as she set it for Jeremy Evans, Ltd.

Tonight, however, her choice of gown was not simply a matter of style. Something made her want to throw the starched white-suited Acheson Lane off his bemused self-confident guard.

Digging in her makeup case, she found the exact shade of eyeshadow to match the dress, but lightened it slightly with white. Since the sunburn gave her skin a glowing tinge, she needed only dark mascara on her already long lashes to provide the finishing touch.

Standing back to gaze at her image in the full-length mirror, she burst out laughing. "I'm just as bad as Mrs. Baldwin and the rest of them! What is it about Acheson Lane that makes a woman pull out all the stops?"

She stopped short and considered the question seriously. Acheson Lane was the first man who had attracted her since Jeremy. Why not have an affair, as Jeremy was always suggesting? She certainly wasn't holding onto her virginity as she had been when she met her husband. Times had changed. Even the strict grandmother who had done so much to form Titania's rigid moral code had passed away five years ago.

It was not the moral question that held her back until now, she knew. She had been keeping herself for Jeremy, hoping he would appreciate her constancy and come back to her. But he had only scoffed at it, taunting her to join the "easy eighties."

"I could jump into a veritable orgy and Jeremy wouldn't care," she bitterly reminded herself. The old hurt crept back into her throat, but she held the tears at bay for fear of ruining her mascara. "Maybe I'm wrong. Maybe he *would* care." The idea returned with force. "What would Jeremy really do if I had an affair?" She had never been unfaithful, not even after the divorce. Her customers were forever bragging about how they purposely made their husbands and lovers jealous just to get them riled up into declaring their love. It had always seemed underhanded and dishonest to Titania; she shrank from using it as a ploy to win back Jeremy.

"What would he do if I told him I had an affair with Acheson Lane?" she mused. He certainly knew enough from Karin Baldwin to be impressed. But would he be *jealous*? Would it goad him into wanting her back?

For the first time in her life, Titania began considering the idea seriously. It was not a ploy she could attempt with just anyone. Acheson Lane sent shivers down her spine. Even if it didn't work on Jeremy, it could be a splendid experience.

But common sense told her the last thing she needed was to get involved with another man like Jeremy. Acheson Lane was obviously cut from the same mold—he'd never be satisfied with just one woman. Rather than fall into the same trap and get hurt again, she knew it would be smarter to forget them both and find a nice guy, maybe not so handsome, but one who would at least be capable of returning her love.

Then again, maybe it was an impossible hope that a man like that existed, and a woman should simply learn how to relate to men with casual indifference. Karin

Baldwin seemed able to juggle an aging husband and a number of lovers without losing sleep over any of them.

With that in mind, she reasoned that Acheson Lane would be a perfect lover. She was already wildly attracted to him. And there was another advantage: After one night she could leave Naupaka and never see him again. It was a foolproof indemnity against getting hurt. He wouldn't have time to do any damage.

And there was always the slim chance that it would make Jeremy wildly jealous and bring him back. That kind of trickery was odious, but hadn't women used it for centuries? Why should she be so aboveboard when slithery women like Karin Baldwin made off with all the men?

She took one last glance in the mirror before walking up to the main building, fully intent on making this night a first, in more ways than one.

To her dismay, Acheson Lane was not waiting for her on the veranda. She had planned a wonderful entrance, gliding up the stairs with the setting sun behind her. She saw the scene in technicolor: the deep purple of the dress, her honey brown hair flowing out, the scarlet sky as her backdrop. But instead of the golden god Acheson Lane, his general manager, Kimo Vasco, was coming toward her.

"Acheson asked me to apologize. Some trouble with the plumbing contractor. He'll be held up for a few minutes. He asked me to give this to you."

Kimo slipped a fragrant flower lei around her neck. The scent was like nothing she had ever experienced, even in the most exclusive salons of Paris. She touched the cool white satin petals. "What kind of flowers are these?"

"Ginger." Kimo had a relaxed easy smile that radiated

brilliantly from his dark face. "It grows wild up in the mountains. That's where it smells the best. It's my favorite kind of flower." Kimo's black eyes were sparkling with mirth. "So you ran into the lifeguard, eh?"

"That was pretty sneaky of you," she teased. "I never expected that he would be Acheson Lane. I don't know why he didn't tell me his real name back then."

Kimo suddenly grew serious. "As a kid, Acheson didn't have it too easy. His parents, well, you probably remember, but you didn't know the half of it. A girl like you—you weren't like some of them who came through here then, and most likely he figured your grandparents would never let you go out with him if they knew he was the Lanes's kid."

"They wouldn't let me go out with him, period. Just the fact that he was a lifeguard!"

"You mean to tell me you sneaked out to meet him?"

She felt some of the old guilt and embarrassment, though she knew it was crazy, twelve years after the fact.

Kimo laughed and slapped his knee. "He never told me that."

"What *did* he tell you?" Had she been too quick to conclude that he had made her the butt of some teenage drinking joke?

"You know something, Mrs. Evans? He never told me anything. No, I'm not kidding. And that's why I remember you. Always before, Acheson and I told each other everything. We grew up together, him and me. We fell off surfboards together, we hiked and got lost in the mountains together. Never any secrets. And you know something else?" Kimo looked at her and smiled in a tender, brotherly way. "We never had any secrets since."

"Oh, he probably just didn't talk about me because he'd put me out of his mind." She tried to make light of what he said, but his words had touched her deeply.

Could it be that Acheson had meant all the wonderful things he had said that night?

Kimo smiled but did not say any more about the subject. "So what you think of this place now?"

"It's quite an impressive atmosphere you've managed to create."

"Me? Don't blame this on me! I liked this old place best when it was closed down and we had it to ourselves. Bring a couple of wahines over from Honolulu and party for two weeks straight. We'd surf and take the canoes out. But Acheson, once he gets an idea into his head, you can't talk sense to him. You just have to go along. Always he's after me to work eighteen-hour days like he does. Crazy, I tell him. What kind of sane person works eighteen hours?"

"I do." Titania laughed.

Kimo threw up his hands. "Maybe if you are in a godforsaken place like Los Angeles I can understand. You work to get out from under the smog. But here? Naupaka? Sometimes I'm sitting at my desk and the waves start to yell at me, 'Hey, Kimo, what you doin' at that desk?'"

"And how do you answer them?"

He shrugged. "I may work for Acheson Lane, but the boss lady? That's the ocean out there. You can't ignore her. She has ways of punishing you. She gets into your mind and torments you till you go to her."

Titania glanced out at the waves splashing on the beach, their mesmerizing rhythm, rolling in, running back out on the sand, teasing and flirting. Only a man with iron willpower could resist. But then, she smiled to herself, Acheson was a *god* of the sea, not her slave.

She watched the large catamaran down on the beach taking on passengers for the sunset sail. What a beautiful time of day to take that ride over the crests of the waves.

Acheson Lane, in his white suit, his blond hair blowing in the trade winds, was coming up the stairs of the veranda. "Sorry I'm late," he apologized. "Has Kimo kept you entertained?"

"Delightfully." She stood up to greet him. It wasn't really necessary to stand up, but she was determined he be treated to the full effect of the purple dress. He took it in in a glance and understood it was for his benefit.

"Thank you for the ginger lei, Acheson. What an amazing fragrance!"

He touched the petals brushing her bare shoulder, the skin silky. He smiled down at her. "It goes well with your dress."

Kimo seemed anxious to be off. "Nice talking to you, Mrs. Evans."

"Please call me Titania."

"Titania! Almost sounds like a Hawaiian name. Have a nice stay!"

Without Acheson having to order, a waiter appeared with a drink and a plate of hors d'oeuvres.

"Do the colors of my sunset suit you, madam?" He made a dramatic gesture out to the sea.

"I believe I ordered red and orange clouds." She played the role of one of her fussy customers.

"They will be arriving any minute, just as soon as that lazy ball of fire dips onto the horizon." He appraised her dress again. "But I'd think that the lavender clouds would go rather well with the dress."

"You sound like a fashion consultant," she teased.

"I've had to be concerned with patterns and colors these last few years," he said seriously in his hotel-owner voice, full of authority.

"Even the sunsets," she said lightly, hoping to distract

him from beginning a business discussion. It had been a long time since she had felt feminine and flirtatious and she was not ready to give it up.

"The Naupaka sunsets never fail me. Ah, there are the colors you ordered, madam."

The change of light came on suddenly, theatrically, and illuminated not only the sky and the sea, but the skin tones of their faces, bathing them in the fiery scarlet light. Acheson was studying her intensely and, remembering what Kimo had said, she found herself growing uncomfortable under his unrelenting gaze. "What are you thinking, Acheson?"

"I was just thinking that there are nuances about a woman—just as there are nuances about the sea."

"For example?" She touched his hand lightly.

"There are unmistakable signs in the way a wave begins to mount before it breaks that tell you it will be a thrilling ride. With a woman, it's the way she tilts her chin, the steady gaze in her eyes, the way she'll punctuate a sentence by touching your hand."

Titania looked away from him, breathing with difficulty. "I suppose you're quite knowledgeable on both subjects." She tried to sound flippant, but knew she didn't.

"There are also waves that give every indication of building magnificently," he continued, forcing her by his will to look at him, "but if you observe carefully, you'll see the ruse. They will take you for a ride, but only a short, disappointing one." He reached across the table and touched her smooth cheek. "What are *you* thinking, princess?"

chapter 7

TITANIA WAS THINKING how much the sunset was like the act of making love: a few spectacular moments that left you awed and breathless—then the long darkness of night closed in. That's how it had been with Jeremy—intense moments of splendor followed by emptiness. And she was annoyed that the vision of her ex-husband had crept into her thoughts like a hovering demon. Perhaps he was like the sea that called to Kimo and she would never be entirely free of him.

It was difficult to carry on a conversation with Acheson Lane while they sipped drinks on the veranda, especially when people began turning back through the lobby toward the dining room for dinner. Everyone, it seemed, felt obliged to stop and exchange a few words. Acheson's open, friendly manner encouraged it. Titania was amazed that he remembered each person's name and where they were from as he introduced her. Some of the people she already knew from Beverly Hills. The women eyed her jealously, taking her presence there with Acheson Lane to mean she was having an affair with him.

The sun took a final bow and left the stage. The spectacle was over, the audience all but cleared the veranda for the dining room. "Are you hungry?" Acheson asked her.

"Famished!"

"We haven't had much time to discuss your store and you're leaving in the morning. I'm afraid if we go into the dining room we'll be constantly interrupted again. Would you consider it too brash if I invited you up to my private suite for dinner?" There were dimples at the edge of his mouth that deepened with humor when he was being droll.

"Brash?" She rested her fingers delicately on his sleeve and gazed boldly into his blue eyes. "Mr. Lane, I understand that to be invited to your suite is quite an honor."

"Honor," he smiled engagingly at her, "has nothing to do with it."

These were flirtatious games Titania had little experience in playing, but she was finding it tantalizing and exciting. For once she could understand Jeremy's fascination with the intricacies of romance. Perhaps she could get used to it—even learn to enjoy it as Jeremy had always suggested.

Two middle-aged women glared at her with blatant envy as she walked across the lobby on Acheson's arm toward his private elevator.

Unlike the airy pastel patterns of the lobby that bore the unmistakable influence of Mrs. Baldwin's decorator, Acheson Lane's penthouse suite was sensuously masculine, entirely his own taste.

On the walls hung bold tapa prints of beige and brown. Vivid green and white Hawaiian-print cushions were strewn across dark rattan furniture. One entire wall opened out onto a large garden balcony where lush scarlet flowers crowded clay pots and fragrant, white-blossomed Plumeria trees grew from huge planters. Beyond was the spreading vista of ocean and sky, now turning dark.

The most extraordinary feature of the penthouse was

the collection of exquisitely carved Polynesian statues. "Most of them are gods of Oceana," he explained. "I've always been fascinated with the legends and culture of this area."

"Who is this grimacing creature?" She stopped in front of the largest statue.

"He's my favorite, the god Maui."

"Isn't Maui one of the Hawaiian Islands?" She touched the smooth, polished wooden surface of the angry-looking tiki.

"The island was named after him."

"And why is it you prefer him to all the others?" Instinctively, she knew it would be the key to Acheson Lane, the part of him that lay hidden to most people.

"Maui was full of mischief, having been raised by dolphins, but he was also a doer of great deeds. He fished these Hawaiian Islands up out of the sea with his fish-hooks, he harnessed the sun and made it promise to go more slowly across the sky, and he brought fire to mankind. He even tried to make mankind immortal by making love to Hine-nui-te-po, this lady over here." He showed her another tiki, a woman with long pendulous breasts, the "Great Lady of Darkness."

"Obviously he didn't succeed at that task," noted Titania, "because we're all still mortal."

"It was his undoing. He lost his life in the effort."

"Poor boy." She patted the tiki's head. "Do you see what trouble you can get into running after ladies of darkness?"

"At least you have to give the guy credit for trying."

Titania was aware again of the determined line of Acheson's jaw, along with the twinkling mischief playing in the depths of his blue eyes. It would be like Acheson Lane to harness the sun. "Now who is this unfortunate creature?" She paused in front of another statue.

"Tangaroa."

She circled around it. "Okay, I give up. Is it male or female? It seems to be extremely well endowed with the attributes of both."

He laughed. "Tangaroa was both male *and* female and was responsible for creating all the gods and humans."

The roar of the ocean carried up to them while the heady scent of Plumerias wafted in on a gentle breeze from the roof garden. In this environment of rich brown tapa prints and bold colors, surrounded by pagan tikis, Titania felt sensual and free. It was the kind of room where one could shed clothes and inhibitions with equal abandon.

But Acheson Lane remained maddeningly aloof, not even removing the white jacket of his suit, though it would have been perfectly natural in his own suite. He made no move toward her that could even be suggestive of a seduction, and Titania reminded herself that she should not expect anything. After all, she was there to discuss business, not a love affair. She herself had made that clear in his office earlier. Nonetheless, a heavy sadness fell over her. Jeremy had spurned her, and now, the first time she began to entertain the possibility of a lover, he didn't even make an attempt to seduce her. She began to wonder if perhaps she was too old for men to consider her appealing.

The dinner arrived via room service, with two efficient waiters in attendance. A darkly polished wooden table near the window was set with fine silver and crystal, blue candles, and white linen. They sat down to eat, and the meal of steak and lobster was served with great flourish. Acheson dismissed the waiters with a wave of his hand: "I think we can handle things from here," he told them, and they quietly disappeared. He took the bottle of wine from the ice bucket and poured them both a glass. "Here's to . . ." He hesitated a moment to find the right toast. Their eyes met and held for a long moment and Titania felt her heart beating to a wild rhythm. What she had not been able to discern before, she now saw eloquently reflected in the depths of his heavy-lidded blue eyes. "Here's to your return to Naupaka," he said softly.

Titania was so stunned by this gesture that she was temporarily without words. "I hope you will consider opening your store here," he continued. The sensuous expression in his eyes suddenly vanished when he mentioned the store. Had she only imagined it? How silly to think that he meant anything other than the store all along.

"We'll certainly give it every consideration," she said pleasantly, hoping he could not see the disappointment she felt. There followed an uncomfortable silence. She broke it at last. "As a little girl, I remember reading about some legends—how the island was forbidden or taboo. What was the story?"

"I'll tell you if it won't discourage you from coming here," he said playfully.

"I'm not in the least superstituious." She tilted her head defiantly. "Go ahead."

"Where to begin," he mused thoughtfully.

"Tell me what happened after Maui fished Naupaka out of the ocean."

"Centuries ago, all the Hawaiian Islands were inhabited by menehunes, little people." His voice became rich and melodic as he warmed to an obviously favorite subject. "Some say they were a pygmy race and others equate them with elves and leprechauns of European folklore. They despised the warlike Polynesian invaders who came across the Pacific in outrigger canoes and they wrought all kinds of mischief in hopes that they'd leave. Finally, most of the menehunes gave up and moved northwest to Naupaka where they engaged the help of a sea god to keep the intruders from invading their island. Terrible things would befall those who tried to make the trip: freak storms, wrecked canoes. Those who made it onto the mysterious island usually met with some strange, unexplained death. So the island was declared off limits—*kapu*, or taboo.

"There was a young prince who angered his father by secretly taking as his wife a girl not of noble blood. They were both to be sacrificed as punishment, but at the last minute the king decided instead to banish them to the forbidden island, Naupaka. The two lovers set out together in a canoe from Kauai in a terrible storm and everyone was sure they would be killed, but the sea god took pity on them and escorted them safely to Naupaka. The menehunes were so moved by their plight that they allowed them to stay and live peacefully among them. But in guiding them to safety, the sea god fell madly in love with the girl, so much in love that he was quite beside himself, and one day while she was swimming, he could no longer contain his passion and stole her away. Her lover was so distraught that he went all over the island, plucking half the petals off the Naupaka flower, and to this day the blossoms, still reflecting his despair, have petals only on one side."

"That's impossible." She looked at him skeptically. "How could there be flowers with petals only on one side?"

He took her hand and led her out onto his roof garden. "You see?" He plucked a blossom from one of his many plants, and she examined it with surprise.

"What a sad story." She understood the tragedy of losing a loved one, and her voice reflected it.

"Not so sad for my family. It was the ancient Hawaiian *kapu* that enabled the Lanes and Achesons from Boston to buy it from King Kamehameha in 1865 for only eight thousand dollars."

"And you rational folk from New England, of course, proved all the silly legends of menehunes to be mere superstitions," she said brightly.

Acheson walked to the edge of the balcony and looked out to sea. "Sometimes I wonder..."

"You don't believe all that, do you?" She looked at him with astonishment.

He leaned up against the balcony wall, his blond hair glowing silver in the moonlight. "Titania, Shakespeare's princess of the fairies, doubts the existence of Hawaiian elves?"

"Not since my grandparents talked me out of my obsession with Santa Claus and the Easter Bunny—though Peter Pan almost made a believer out of me. You have to admit Tinker Bell is a compelling character."

He grew serious. "I wish I could tell you we all lived happily ever after here, but it would not be true. We've had terrible luck. Crops failed for no apparent reason; cattle died. The first Achesons and Lanes died violent deaths—freak 'accidents,' you could say. The family has been plagued with mysterious illnesses. It was only because the plantation was failing so badly that my grandparents decided to open a resort here."

"But that prospered," she protested. "My grandparents told me about it."

"It prospered for a few years," he explained. "Then my grandparents died and my parents took over management...you must remember what a catastrophe that was. Then one night, the car they were driving careened over a cliff. Of course, they had been drinking heavily..." His voice trailed off.

Titania was visibly moved by his story. "I'm sure all those things could be explained rationally," she said softly. "Acheson, you don't *really* believe there is something supernatural, a kind of curse on your family?"

He shrugged. "Mere chance? Coincidence? Bad luck?"

"Perhaps the first Achesons and Lanes didn't know much about farming methods in the tropics. After all, the climate is quite different from New England. Everyone is prone to tropical fevers of one kind or another. And the resort would have done well if it had been managed correctly."

He took her arm and led her back into the room. "Well, at least you know the drawbacks of opening a store here." His dimples showed.

"For a moment there I thought you really did believe in evil spirits and little menehunes!"

He poured her another glass of wine. "If I believed in evil spirits, would I be making this kind of investment in Naupaka?"

"*You'd* probably do it just to defy the little fellows!"

"You're probably right." As he smiled she was once again aware of the firm chiseled lines of his face. "My father used to carry on miserably about the 'luck of the Lanes,' as though we were swimming helplessly in the middle of the Pacific without a lifeboat in sight. But I don't think fate tosses you about on the waves. I think you make your own luck. And Naupaka, with the right management, the right publicity, the right stores . . ."

He had been talking with an electric intensity that awed her. She traced her long, graceful fingers across the scowling carved face of Maui and looked up at Acheson. "Of course, if *he* could harness the sun . . ."

Acheson threw back his head and laughed. "You're the first person to come up here who has realized why I keep that ugly guy around. He's a constant reminder that you can pull islands up out of the sea."

"I don't have the slightest doubt you'll do it, Acheson," she said with an almost breathless admiration. She had never known that kind of feeling for anyone before and it startled her. It was as though she were confronting the great Maui himself.

"We can't miss with your store in the arcade, Titania."

"You've got it!" She could have refused him nothing at that moment, least of all her store.

"You mean it?"

"Yes."

"Wonderful!" He threw his arms around her. She knew it was only an impulsive hug, a friendly gesture to celebrate her decision, but she was intensely aware of the mysterious feelings radiating between them. She had not felt that way since he had held her in his arms on that beach so many years ago.

Did he feel it too? He let her go almost at once, but their eyes held. She longed to ask him, but she was struck speechless by the tremors that still shook her body.

He started to say something but instead drew her close. His lips touched her forehead, her cheek. "Titania," he murmured huskily in her ear, "it's going to be wonderful having you here."

But just as his lips found hers, she jerked away. This is what she had promised Jeremy to avoid. She was being swept away by her emotions, acting impulsively. Having a love affair with this captivating man was one thing, doing business with him quite another. How had she managed to confuse the two? Jeremy would be furious that she'd used so little judgment. Oh, damn Jeremy! The rage mounted in her chest as the thought of him edged between her and Acheson. Why must I always consider Jeremy? Why can't I be free of this choking, strangulating love for him?

Acheson was studying her quietly. "That was wrong

of me," he apologized suddenly. "I know how you feel about mixing business and pleasure. You made that clear to me this morning."

"It's my fault, too," she said nervously. "I was giving you the impression that I would . . . well, that I wanted . . ."

"Well, let's forget that little relapse and have another drink to celebrate the opening of Jeremy Evans, Ltd. at Naupaka."

It irritated Titania that he could remain so aloof and unshaken by their contact, when she was still trembling from his touch. "Thanks, Acheson, but I'd better be going," she answered briskly, lifting her chin. "I'm leaving early tomorrow morning. I'll have our lawyer get in touch with yours and they can have a wonderful time mulling over the fine print of the lease agreements." There was still time to slip out of her decision to open a store there, but oddly, she felt no remorse about it. She was certain she would have come to the same conclusion despite her turbulent feelings for him.

"Let me see you back to your bungalow," he suggested, pressing the button for his private elevator."

"That's all right. I'm not afraid of the menehunes," she said lightly.

"Then what is it you fear, princess?"

She would not meet his penetrating gaze, for if she did, she knew she could not resist throwing herself in his strong arms again. The elevator door opened and she stepped in quickly. "Thank you for a lovely evening, Acheson. See you in the morning before I leave."

The door began to close but Acheson held it open. "You didn't answer my question."

"Avoiding it was an answer of sorts," she said evasively.

He suddenly grinned. "An eloquent answer, I might add. Rest assured, I won't burden you with any relapses.

It was just curiosity. I wanted to see if holding you in my arms was as good as I remember."

She lifted her eyes, her own curiosity about what he felt outweighing any other reservations. "Well, was it?"

"Some answers are more eloquent when they are not direct, princess." His dark blue eyes sparkled with a wicked smile as he let the elevator door close.

She cursed him under his breath as the elevator descended to the lobby. She was astute enough to know he was tantalizing her.

Her mind reeled with a dozen ways to get back at him. In one of her scenarios, she thought of going back up in the elevator, arriving at his floor stark naked, then closing the door on him before he could reach her. However amusing it might be, she knew she hadn't the nerve to pull off anything so outrageous!

Walking down the garden path to the bungalow, she stole a glance up at the roof garden. He was there, looking like a carved statue, staring out at the sea, his hair tinted silver by the moonlight and blowing about his chiseled face in the trade winds.

As she lay on the wide bed in her bungalow, Titania glanced through the paperback novel she had bought at the Los Angeles airport, but the words were blurring as her mind raced over the events of the last day.

She saw the unfinished arcade where her store would be and mentally rearranged it to suit her needs. She thought about what kind of clothes she would have to stock: bolder colors and lighter fabrics than for Beverly Hills. She would have to get in touch with some of the Hawaiian manufacturers. She had seen some women with beautiful things like wrapshorts, that could only have come from Hawaii.

Suddenly the image of Mrs. Baldwin flashed before

her eyes. Titania remembered the dress the woman had insisted on buying—a stunning dark brown silk, but a ghastly color for a woman with olive skin. Mrs. Baldwin, against her usual good judgment, had argued that she must have brown. "It goes with a particular decor I want to fit into," she had said mysteriously. What she had meant, Titania was sure now, was the brown of Acheson's tapa prints. What a stupid thing to do, Titania yawned. Who would want to fade into a wall? It made no sense.

A woman should always try to stand out from a background, not blend into it. She thought of several dresses she would recommend to Mrs. Baldwin when she returned to Beverly Hills. The strapless red silk with the yellow sash, the blue crepe with the scalloped hem, the . . . Titania paused in her reverie. Mentally, she was dressing herself in these clothes, dazzling the scowling tiki gods in Acheson Lane's suite.

Acheson Lane. How many turbulent emotions he had aroused in her! Awe, passion, sympathy, and admiration. She went over again what he had said about building Naupaka. With that kind of determination—he was right—the hotel could not lose. She felt justified in having decided to open the store there. Jeremy could not accuse her of letting her heart rule her on that score.

It was odd, she thought, how much gnawing love she felt for Jeremy, and yet never had she been awed by him. Never had she felt even the slightest admiration.

Her love for Jeremy had eaten away at her heart, wrenched buckets of tears from swollen eyes, but it had all emanated from a powerful, undefinable physical source. It had not come from esteem. In fact, she realized that, had she not been married to him, she might never have considered him worthy as a business partner. She had never been blind to his faults, his lack of scruples, but love had overpowered her judgment.

There was a breeze from the window, blowing in the warm night winds from off the sea. Without bothering to slip on a bathrobe, she went out to the lanai, her filmy nightgown fluttering gently around her in the wind, outlining her slender body. It was close to midnight, the same hour she had slipped over that same wall so many years ago.

A man was on the moonlit beach, walking toward the water for a swim. He looked back for a moment. Afraid that she had been seen, she moved under the shadow of a tall fern, out of the glaring moonlight.

He began to jog toward the ocean, the blond mane of his hair flowing back from his face. Unrestricted now by his gentlemanly white suit, Acheson's broad shoulders relaxed as he ran in long even strides on the sand. The closer he came to the water's edge, the faster was his pace until he was sprinting, leaping over the foam. A wave curled up before him and he hurled himself into it like a spear, disappearing into the night.

Titania's chest was tight, suffocating from the pressure of longing that filled her body. Turning back to her room, she shut the door, but the heady fragrance of the salt air mingling with ginger blossoms seeped into her consciousness.

With the brash recklessness of a seventeen-year-old girl, she grabbed her bathing suit, still damp enough from her afternoon swim to harden the nipples on her softly rounded breasts. She was breathing with difficulty, ready to explode as she raced down to the beach, her long, honey brown hair loose and flowing out behind her like the tail of a comet.

She saw him emerge from the surf, his skin glistening

in the moonlight with sequins of sea spray, his hair washed silver by the moon's rays. As she stood waiting for him, the sea gently reached up and caressed her ankles.

chapter 8

As HE CAME toward her she began to feel foolish at having run after him. "Nice night for a swim," he said casually with a grin.

"Yes. It is. I had no idea you'd be down here." She lied awkwardly.

"Of course, you didn't." He threw back his leonine head and laughed. "I saw you watching me from your bungalow."

Caught in her lie, she smiled shyly at him.

"Well, come on, if you want to swim." He took her hand and led her into the water.

She had forgotten how warm the tropical Pacific was. Letting go of his hand, she dove under a wave. He followed. Like two sleek dolphins, they moved silently together through the dark water. When they were quite a ways from shore beyond the breakers, they stopped to tread water and let the rolling waves lift them up and down.

"Do you always come out this time of night?" she asked him.

"It's the only time I can get any privacy out here unless I go to one of the other beaches on the island, but there's little time for that now with all the building. Are you tired yet?"

"Not yet." She lay on her back and gazed up at the

stars. "Besides, I don't have to worry with a lifeguard beside me, do I?"

"It's been years since I saved anyone's life. Better not count on me," he joked.

She knew better. Wtih him at her side she felt at peace, protected. Nothing bad could befall her as long as he was there.

The moon reflected on the water like a pathway of shimmering silver coins. In the distance they could see the tiny lights of the white hotel cradled in palm trees. What an ideal life, she was thinking dreamily, to live at a beautiful resort, to have a handsome lover to swim with in the moonlight.

They were slowly, silently drifting with the currents when he suggested they start back. "There's a coral reef just down there. We don't want to get too close."

She felt pleasantly exhausted as they neared shore and was grateful to feel the hard pebbly sand under her feet and Acheson's strong arm holding hers for balance as they came out of the water. She glanced up at him to smile and was momentarily surprised at how tall he was. When she had walked alongside him earlier, she had been wearing high heels. "Let me buy you a drink," he offered.

"We can't go into the hotel bar like this, can we?"

"No. They'd throw us out. I'll get us something from the bar down here at the beach."

"Isn't it closed at this hour?"

"When you're the owner, they tell you where they hide the key. It's very convenient."

He went behind the bar and, taking a couple of bottles, walked back with her to the bungalow.

Titania's heart was pounding with anticipation. The sight of Acheson Lane, the long muscled legs, blond hair curling up under his swim trunks, aroused feelings she had long ago suppressed.

While he went to the small kitchenette to fix them drinks, she wondered if she should change out of her bathing suit, but into what? With a kind of terror, she realized that she had never, ever had a love affair. After a few brief, chaste bumbling romances, she had been married. There were rules of etiquette for these situations, outlined meticulously in modern books and magazines she had never bothered to read.

Before she could come to a decision about the bathing suit, he was handing her the drink. "Why don't we go out on the terrace," she suggested. "I wouldn't want to ruin your beautiful new decor with our wet suits."

"Then let's take them off," he said logically.

"Just like that?"

"No, we could always wait and see if they disintegrate with our own body heat."

"Don't laugh at me, Acheson. I'm not very experienced at all this—I mean, I don't know exactly what you're supposed to do. It just seems so crass to stand here and strip down naked. Is that what you usually do?"

Acheson chuckled and, taking her hand, led her out to the patio. "No, that's not what we're going to do. In fact, we don't *have* to do anything if you don't want to. Just say the word and I'll leave. We've had a nice swim and now we're having a pleasant drink. Just look up at those stars and take a deep breath of that air." He stretched his huge frame out in a lounge chair and took a long sip from his glass. "Salt water makes you thirsty," he observed.

Titania was wishing he weren't so agreeable. He seemed hardly to care whether they made love or not. Did he have any idea of the trauma she had brought on herself by running down to meet him tonight? She had geared up for a passionate night of love, and yet he seemed perfectly content to lie back and look up at the stars.

She was standing a few feet away from him, wondering what to do when he slipped his large hand around her thigh, caressing the soft inner skin with his thumb. "Come here, fairy princess."

She sat down on the edge of the chaise facing him. He was smiling up at her. Her long hair had been swept back behind her ears when she had come out of the ocean, and now he took it gently and brought it forward to frame her oval face, caressing her smooth shoulders. "You should always wear your hair long," he said softly. His sea blue eyes worshipped her with a tenderness that drew her breath away.

She was still holding her drink awkwardly. He removed it from her hand and placed it on the ground, then drawing her face down to his, he kissed her, lightly at first, savoring the taste of a moment so long awaited. Anxious as she was to kiss him fully, he would not rush it.

As she began to respond, he ruffled his strong fingers through her hair, drawing it back tightly, pressing her to him with increasing passion.

His hands moved down her sides, pulling the top of her bathing suit down to her waist. The tips of her breasts were aroused by feeling the coarse hair of his muscled chest. He was lifting her hips, moving her on top of him, and she felt his demanding hardness.

He was pulling her bathing suit down further over her slender hips, when suddenly she stiffened. "We're out here in the open," she whispered. "Anyone could see us, Acheson."

"We're hidden by the foliage," he assured her. "But if you'd rather we went inside . . . we'd be more comfortable, that's for sure."

"Yes, let's go inside," she said shakily.

She darted up, but her legs were weak as she tried to

walk across the room. Her bathing suit was half off, exposing her breasts, and she was about to pull it up modestly when she saw Acheson standing at the door watching her through heavy-lidded, sultry eyes. "My god, but you're beautiful, princess," he whispered.

They sprawled out across the large bed and, straddling her on his knees, he quickly removed the clinging bathing suit. She yielded to the caress of his warming gaze then to the gentle kisses that paid homage to her smooth naked skin.

His caressing lips and hands wandered and explored the soft contours of her eager body, finding all the hidden, sensitive recesses that made her twist and moan with waves of mounting pleasure.

She longed to discover all the mysteries of this huge, golden god who tasted like the sea.

"My princess," he murmured as she wrapped her long legs around his strong back.

She remembered the other princess of Naupaka who had been captured by the sea god. The story was not so sad after all, she thought wildly as she drifted down with him below the rolling waves, swirling, plunging deeper into the blue silky darkness. It was not like the fiery sunset that was over in a few glowing moments. It went on and on, consuming, renewing, hurling them into the emerald depths, crashing down with crystal white breakers.

She gazed around at the room beginning to fill with yellow ribbons of dawn. Sheets and pillows had been scattered helter-skelter to the floor. His trunks had been flung over a chair, her bathing suit hung limply over the headboard of the bed. "It looks like a hurricane went through here," she whispered to Acheson, who held her cradled in his strong arm.

"You mean you missed it?"

She kissed the warm hollow of his neck, still damp from the heat of their lovemaking. It tasted deliciously of the sea. "Cannons could have been fired off in this room and I wouldn't have heard them."

He hugged her and she felt again the shudders of passion that had wracked her body all night. "Are you happy, princess?" He kissed her forehead. She nodded. "When you open your store here, you can move into my suite and we'll make love like this every night."

The store. She had forgotten all about the store. How could she possibly open the store here after this? It had been hard enough running a business with an ex-husband.

"There are enchanted places on Naupaka I want you to see, Titania, we'll..."

"I'm not opening the store here," she interrupted him.

He moved himself around to look at her directly to see if she was joking. She was not.

"But when you left my place after dinner, it was all settled. I don't understand."

She sat up in bed, her long hair falling forward on her face. She brushed it nervously from her eyes. "Acheson, it's impossible now. I can't be both your mistress and your business associate. It doesn't work."

"Anything can work for us," he said stubbornly.

"Not this..." Her mind was whirling. Was she only putting him off to protect herself from his eventual rejection? Or was it Jeremy? How could she have given herself over so completely to this man when her heart still ached for Jeremy? The guilt began to haunt her. Jeremy was the only man who had ever made love to her before this night. How could she have managed to betray him so completely?

Acheson took her head in his large, strong hands. "Then to hell with the store. I don't want you to be my mistress *or* my business associate, Titania."

She looked at him with confusion. "But what else is there?"

"I want you to be my wife."

She pulled away from him abruptly as though he had slapped her. "But I *can't* be your wife."

"Why not?" A man who could raise islands out of the sea was not easily turned away.

"I just can't!" she cried. She was still Jeremy's wife— not legally, of course. But what did a piece of paper mean when she still loved him as her husband. Acheson Lane would never understand that. But Acheson's wife! He couldn't be serious. Why was he tormenting her with such insanity? "Please, Acheson, don't play with me."

He grabbed her shoulders roughly. "Titania, I'm not playing. I've loved you since the first moment I saw you."

"That's the stuff of fairy tales! No man nurtures a love for so many years. Passion is a fleeting thing. You'll forget all about me as soon as I'm out of your sight."

"Titania, will you listen to what I'm saying?" His frustration was close to anger. "I want to *marry* you!"

"You probably tell that to all your mistresses to make them love you more." As soon as she said it, she saw the fury blaze in his sapphire eyes.

"I've never said that to any woman before." His deep voice shook with emotion as his lips came down on hers.

"Acheson, Acheson," she moaned as her own passion exploded again within her. She would straighten out her thoughts in the clear light of day. For the moment, there was nothing to do but abandon herself to the raging need he roused within her.

chapter 9

THE CESSNA CITATION touched ground and taxied to a halt on the airstrip that served the Naupaka plantation and hotel. Having connected in Honolulu with flights from the mainland, the small jet would be bringing in new hotel guests as well as taking out those returning to Honolulu.

Titania watched it nervously, unable to lift her eyes to meet Acheson's. "Stay just a few more days, Titania."

She shook her head. "We had one wonderful night. If I leave now, there will be no bad feelings."

"At least reconsider opening your store here," he suggested.

"I couldn't now, not after last night."

"You managed to maintain a business partnership with your husband after a marriage. Why should this be any different?" he asked reasonably.

"Don't you see, Acheson? That's how I *know* it doesn't work. It's very painful to work with someone, to shut out all emotions, when you still love him."

The airplane door opened and the passengers began to descend. With surprise, Titania saw that Karin Baldwin was among them.

Acheson grabbed Titania's hand and swung her around to meet his gaze. "Now I understand." His face flushed with anger under his tan. "It has nothing to do with me or opening a store. Why didn't you tell me last night you were still in love with your ex-husband?"

"I don't know. I suppose I wanted you to think I was as flippant and unconcerned about that relationship as when we talked in your office."

"So last night was just a little tropical moonlight fling." Acheson was seething with rage. "I suppose you'll go back to Mr. Evans and tell him all the details to make him jealous. That's what women usually do. Good ploy, Titania. I'm sure it will work. It will kill him to think of you in another man's arms."

"Please don't be angry, Acheson," she said, miserable.

"No, of course not," he said with sarcasm. "I bare my soul to you and you don't even have the guts to tell me you're in love with your ex-husband. You're right. It's best we part here."

"Mrs. Evans, darling, and Acheson, dear." Karin Baldwin's low voice interrupted them. "How cozily familiar you two seem to be. I couldn't help but notice as I got off the plane. May I speak to you for a moment, Mrs. Evans?"

"Uh, sure," said Titania, following her back toward the plane. She was secretly grateful for an excuse to get away from Acheson's rage.

Karin Baldwin was not a woman of many words when only a few would suffice. "Keep your hands off him," she seethed. "Open a store here if you want, but don't forget that Acheson Lane is *mine*."

Titania blinked with surprise. "Funny, I didn't see the ring in his nose with your initials on it."

"I mean it," said Mrs. Baldwin with a scowl that distorted her flawless aristocratic features.

Titania was shocked by the vehemence. "I've never

known you to be that possessive of any man."

"Acheson Lane isn't just 'any man,' though it looks as though you've already found that out. He might fool around with you, it's only natural. There's no way to keep him away from women completely. But his ties to me are much deeper than you imagine."

"You don't seem very sure of yourself." Titania couldn't resist goading her.

"I have reasons to be extremely sure of myself. Acheson's a great one with pretty words. He probably filled you up with all sorts of lovely fantasies. That's why women like him. But I know where his heart is, my dear. Believe me, I know."

Acheson was coming swiftly toward them. Had he lied to her last night? What would have been the motivation?

She knew it shouldn't matter as long as she was still in love with Jeremy, but what Karin Baldwin said stung her, nonetheless.

"Titania," he said, placing a hand on her shoulder. She looked up at him with confusion.

Karin Baldwin was glaring at her.

Suddenly, Titania did not want to abandon Acheson and the island of Naupaka. For the first time she was uncertain of her love for Jeremy.

People were boarding the airplane.

"There is still time to reconsider," he told her. His anger seemed to have subsided.

"You musn't pressure her into opening a store here, Acheson, darling," said Karin Baldwin acidly.

Titania glanced from Acheson to Karin, her heart pounding.

The last passengers were aboard. "I believe the plane is waiting for you," said Karin Baldwin.

Suddenly she began to shake with rage, realizing what

Karin Baldwin had just had the audacity to demand! Here
was a woman who had suffered no moral scruples about
flirting with her husband in front of the salesgirls, calling
him at home to make dates while they were still married,
flaunting her affair with Jeremy at every opportunity.
And now she presumed to demand Titania leave Acheson
Lane.

Even in the thick of Jeremy's affair, Titania had refused to lower her pride and confront the other woman,
Karin, and demand that she not see Jeremy. Of course,
it had been simply one more in a long line of his affairs
that she had suffered.

But now Karin Baldwin's threat concerning Acheson
had the opposite effect from what she intended. Mrs.
Baldwin did not own Acheson Lane any more than the
mythical menehunes owned Naupaka. Titania refused to
be intimidated.

As she gazed at Acheson, the night came back to her
in a rush, mingling memories with her first trip to Naupaka. It all seemed unreal, something she had conjured
up. Sure, she could stay and fight Karin Baldwin for
possession of his soul, but then what?

Jeremy Evans, not Acheson Lane or Karin Baldwin,
was the crux of all her problems. She could not hope to
begin anything new until she came to terms with her love
for Jeremy. A store, even a passionate love affair, on
Naupaka was no escape.

She extended her hand to Acheson and lifted her chin
in a gesture of determination to control her own destiny.
"I will let you know," she told him evenly.

"I'll call you tonight," he answered quickly.

chapter 10

EXHAUSTED FROM A sleepless, active night and the long
flight from Honolulu, Titania was glad her condominium
was not far from Los Angeles International Airport.
Other than for its proximity to the airport and the ocean,
she hated the high-rise building that had become hers in
the divorce settlement. She hated Marina del Rey.

It had been Jeremy's idea to live there, not because
he liked sailing or being near the sea, but because the
weather was often foggy and damp, reminding him of
his hometown, London. And there was a fine collection
of young professional "beautiful" people who populated
the cubicles of the high-rise boxes that dominated the
landscape more forcefully than the slender masts of sail-
boats and yachts. But as much as she loathed it, Jeremy
loved it. After putting in twelve hours at the store, he
could come home, shower, be the life of a party, and
still be fresh for work the next morning. Titania couldn't.
And after the first year of marriage she gave up trying.

Looking back, she realized that letting Jeremy go off
to Marina parties alone was probably a mistake—though
she didn't know how she could have stopped him. He
had always been sociable. She had met him at a designer's party in New York, and it was his suave, witty
manner that had attracted her to him.

Before she even had a chance to unpack, the doorbell rang. Jeremy was still in his suit and tie, just coming back from work. "Hi, duckie, how'd it go?" He went to the liquor cabinet and mixed himself a drink with an annoying familiarity. "Couldn't have been all work and no play. You're red as a lobster. What's that perfume— whew, it's strong!"

"It's not perfume, it's a ginger lei. Did those silk blouses come in yet from New York?" She desperately wanted to avoid talking about the trip.

"No." He made himself comfortable on the couch, loosening his tie. "I called them this morning at seven our time and they keep saying they're on the way. Bloody liars, if you ask me."

"Maybe we should stop ordering from New York," she mused. "At least from Dallas they pay the freight."

"I agree." He laughed. She and Jeremy were never in disagreement when it came to the business. Ideas flowed in natural progression. At times she could still look at him with a certain detachment, unmoved by the slender, dark good looks. Jeremy sported style as though he had just stepped out of the pages of *Esquire*. Unconsciously, she began comparing him to Acheson Lane.

Though Jeremy wore clothes well, he had little muscle tone. She suspected his aversion to outdoor activities had a great deal to do with not wanting to expose his thin legs and narrow chest to ridicule.

"Baldwin was getting off the plane this morning as I was getting on," Titania informed him.

"I saw her last night," he said casually. "She thinks a store at this Naupaka is a terrific idea, even if she did mastermind it herself. She seems to think this Acheson Lane character is quite a guy, too."

The mention of his name caused her heart to jump as she recalled images of their lovemaking the night before.

"He's got a computer brain." She spoke quickly, trying to cover up her agitation. "Knows everything about everybody. Effusively charming. It's a beautiful resort. No doubt about it."

"So you think we ought to go with it?"

"No, not at all," she stammered. "I think it's risky."

"Risky? Baldwin didn't seem to think so. And I would suspect, though she won't admit it, that the Baldwin Bank didn't think so either. I bet they've laid a lot of money into that venture. You said yesterday that we'd be the only women's clothing store in there. How could we lose?"

She had to think quickly. Jeremy would never accept as an excuse that she had just had a torrid night of love. He had no such scruples about mixing sex and business. For a moment, she dallied with the idea of telling him about the curse of the menehunes. Jeremy would find it amusing, but he was the kind of man who walked under ladders and dared black cats to cross his path.

"It's an isolated island, away from the mainstream of tourism," she said finally. "It's priced for a very exclusive market. Right now it is successful, but it's also small. He'll have to keep up the same service with the new section he's building. Possibly he can, but if he doesn't, we could go under with him. Also, we'd have to take out another loan to make the investment. We're still paying off the first loan we made to put in the Beverly Hills store."

"But, my dear, going into debt is the 'Ameddican way.'" He exaggerated his English accent. "Think of the tax advantages."

"Of going bankrupt?" she scoffed.

"What a pessimist you are. Yesterday you were ready to sell your soul to get us into Naupaka."

She ran her fingers through her long hair nervously.

"I simply think we should weigh the pros and cons. No sense in diving headfirst into this. If we do invest over there, it's going to be up to me to run that store. I already know how *you* feel about the tropics."

"And *you* are the one always extolling its virtues," he reminded her. "When we were married you were always begging me to take you to Hawaii or Acapulco for a vacation. Not that I wouldn't miss your smiling face every day in Beverly Hills." He was being sarcastic, but there was a tenderness in his voice that she knew was sincere. Whatever else their relationship had degenerated into, their work days were still good. "Listen, luv, I'm on my way to a party in Pacific Palisades. Would you like to come?" He was appraising her with the dark-eyed look that had once made her forgive everything and race into his arms despite the worst revelations about his love affairs. She was still susceptible to the undeniable charm of her ex-husband. There was a soft, vulnerable place in her heart that he could always penetrate with that dark look. She hated her weakness for it.

"No, Jer, I've got to unpack," she said with difficulty. She knew what those evenings were like—watching Jeremy flirt with half a dozen women.

"I didn't think you'd go. You never do. I don't know why I bother to ask. Habit, I guess."

"It's a habit I wish you'd break." She was suddenly irritated. Who was he to barge into her condominium uninvited, fix himself a drink, and put his feet up on the coffee table as if he still lived here?

"If you went to a party now and then, you might meet someone, luv." He was enjoying provoking her temper.

"Much as I know it would relieve your sense of guilt, Jeremy, I'm sorry but I'm just not interested in meeting anyone," she snapped.

"You can't play the wronged woman gone to live out

the rest of her lonely days in a nunnery all your life. Don't forget, I know you better than that. You're not cut out for the celibate life." .

"Your tender concern is touching," she said bitterly, "but my personal life is no longer your business."

"It could be." He raised his dark eyebrows. "I never wanted a divorce, remember."

"But you never wanted to be married, either." Anger was bubbling to the surface while her heart was turning over.

"Not in the traditional sense. If you'd only been a bit more open-minded..."

"Jeremy," she managed through clenched teeth. "Let's not get into that again." Her cheeks were flushed with rage. If only I didn't still love him, she thought with anguish, I could listen to him talk like that and it wouldn't bother me.

These arguments had never bothered him in the least. He shrugged it off with indifference. "Okay. See you at the store tomorrow, luv."

She sank down at the kitchen table. The cold fog she hated was rolling in and enveloping the tall block of impersonal cubicles across the way. How much more at home she had felt in the warmth of her Naupaka bungalow. Her airline ticket was lying on the table and she began sketching absently on the back of it until it suddenly became a floor plan for the new store.

What did she really have that would hold her in Los Angeles? Her grandparents were dead. Jeremy was giving her nothing but grief. The Beverly Hills store was like a child who had grown up. Other than buying for it, which she could still do several times a year, Jeremy could run it quite well alone.

Naupaka was a new adventure, a new challenge, and one that would take her miles away from Jeremy and the daily heartbreak she had to face with him. If there was any truth in the old adage, "out of sight, out of mind," now was the time to find out.

If only Acheson Lane weren't part of the bargain, it would be perfect. With sudden revelation, she realized that she'd forgotten all about her resolve to taunt Jeremy into jealousy with her affair. She hadn't even hinted at it. Was it because she still wanted him to think she was faithful to him?

Titania felt her body shudder as she remembered Ancheson's lovemaking. She would never tell Jeremy— it had nothing to do with Jeremy. It was her secret—hers and Acheson's. They might never see each other again, but they would always have their exquisite experiences to remember.

The phone rang. Her hand trembled as she answered and recognized Acheson's deep resonant voice, though it sounded uncharacteristically thin coming from so many miles. "I wanted to apologize for what I said this morning at the airport. I had no right to make demands on you, Titania. What is between you and your ex-husband is none of my business, but I would still like you to consider opening the store here. You and I can have an understanding—strictly a business association. You can trust me to hold to that."

Titania experienced a vague disappointment. She would have preferred his passion, a renewal of his marriage offer—even though accepting would have been out of the question. Her sagging ego needed a boost at the moment, and Acheson seemed only too easily persuaded to halt his pursuit of her. But then Karin Baldwin was there now.

"What does Jeremy think of opening up here?"

"He will go along with whatever I decide." For some reason, she didn't want to tell him Jeremy had just been there. "Can you give me about a week to make up my mind?"

"I would love to give you a year, Titania, but unfortunately I have two other stores wanting an answer from me right away. My first choice, as I told you, is Jeremy Evans, Ltd. It has the style I envision for Naupaka. But if you feel that you can't, I'll understand."

With the same reckless spirit that had sent her flying down to the beach to meet him the night before, she said, "Well, all right then. Let's go for it."

There was a brief silence on his end of the line. "Good," he answered finally, his voice betraying no emotion she could detect. "How soon can you be ready to open?"

She made a quick calculation. "Six to eight weeks. I'll do my buying here then fly back to Naupaka to get everything in order. Send me the architect's floor plan of the store so I can begin organizing the layout."

"It will be in tomorrow's mail. You'll have your lawyer send me the contracts?"

His voice was crisply businesslike. Titania mused that she could have been a man for all the emotion he put into the conversation. But she was grateful for it. It would be better this way, she knew.

"We'll sign and get them right back to you," she assured him. "Oh, one more thing, I'll need a place to stay on Naupaka."

"I'll have a room for you at the hotel, no problem."

"Isn't that rather an imposition?"

"You could board at an old farmhouse. That's the only other structure on the island, but I'm sure you'll be more comfortable at the hotel. It's no imposition. I'm delighted you reconsidered. Call me collect if you have any questions. See you soon. Aloha."

"Aloha." She barely had a chance to get the word out before she heard the click of his end. She sighed. It would definitely *not* be the same between them.

chapter 11

ACHESON WAS ON a business trip to Honolulu when she arrived at Naupaka, but she was surprised and delighted to learn that number twelve had been set aside for her exclusive use. Kimo told her with a wink that it had not been rented since she left, by Acheson's orders.

The second night, Acheson was back at the resort and invited her to have dinner with him, this time in the formal main dining room. They shared a table with a charming Italian opera star and his French wife.

"Is there anything I can do for you?" Acheson asked as he escorted her back to the bungalow that night. She was relieved he was acting the role of the professional hotel owner, treating her with no more or less polite familiarity than he would any business associate.

"No, thanks, everything is fine. Well, there are some things at the store, but I can discuss them with you tomorrow." She considered inviting him in for a drink but then thought better of it. It would be best to keep things on an affable impersonal level.

"By the way, since you're going to be spending some time with us, you really should get acquainted with the Vascos, Kimo's parents. His father has run the plantation since before I was born. Kimo and I are going over there to dinner tomorrow night, if you'd like to join us."

It was an innocent enough invitation. "I'd love to. It would be nice to get acquainted with some of the people who live here."

"I'm afraid besides the hotel staff and plantation workers, there aren't many permanent residents on Naupaka," he said apologetically. "I hope you won't be bored here. The social life will be quite different from Los Angeles."

"I wouldn't have come if I didn't expect my life here to be very different," she assured him.

He put a hand on her arm and his warm touch made her tremble. She pulled away from it. "It's very kind of you to include me in your party tomorrow night," she said stiffly, hoping he couldn't see the trauma his touch had caused.

"You're part of the Naupaka family now." He gave her a beguiling grin, then added on a formal note, "We want you to feel at home."

She knew she should be grateful for his civility. There could be no complaint about his decorum. But inside, she melted every time her eyes met his deep blue ones, and she imagined him without his white suit, the tanned, muscled body stretched out on the bed next to her.

There were still nagging doubts about her decision to open the store on Naupaka. Acheson was making it clear he did not want to resume their affair, and it should have put her at ease. Now she wondered if she hadn't gone from the frying pan into the fire in exchanging her business relationship with Jeremy Evans for an equally disturbing one with Acheson Lane.

And though she felt extreme agitation in the presence of both these men, she knew that there was a subtle difference. She tried to pinpoint it as she lay in her bed that night. Undoubtedly a psychiatrist would find something sexual behind it, but while Jeremy usually brought out her fury, Acheson seemed to strike a dissonant chord that jarred rather than angered. She mused that if one were to observe her reactions on a silent film, there would probably be no difference to be seen in the actual physical effects. But inside she knew it was not the same.

The next night she met Acheson and Kimo in the parking lot. They took one of the Naupaka jeeps for the bumpy ride over the dirt roads to the plantation. "Eventually, I'm going to have to pave more roads than simply the one from the airstrip to the hotel," Acheson explained, "but my main concern right now is getting the new building completed."

As they drove through the sugar cane fields, Acheson and Kimo explained the farming methods to her, then amused her by describing how they used to play hide-and-seek there as children.

The white wooden ranch house sprawled lazily out over a green hill, partially hidden by thick shrubs and shade trees.

"The original ranch house from the 1850s is hidden in there somewhere, but there've been so many additions over the years, nobody knows anymore what the original one looked like," Acheson explained. His grandparents, she learned, were the last of the Acheson and Lane families to live at the ranch. Once the hotel had been built, they left the ranch house to the plantation managers.

Henry Vasco, Kimo's father, was just driving up in his pickup truck as they approached the house.

A wiry, dark-skinned man of Portuguese descent, with white hair, Papa Vasco had a broad easy smile that lit up his narrow face and brightened his black eyes. His wife was a mixture of island races. She had long ago given up the fight to stay slender and now plumply filled out the long muu-muu she wore. But she was beautiful nonetheless, with a wide smile and twinkling eyes. A gentle warmth emanated from her as she hugged them all, including Titania. "I'm so happy to meet you. We've heard all about you and the lovely store you're going to open. Please excuse my house: it's always a mess. Too many kids running in and out all day, and I figure, what the heck, who wants to be cleaning and scolding all the time, eh?"

Although most of the Vasco children, like Kimo, were grown, several of the older ones continued to live in the huge house with their wives or husbands and children so that people were constantly popping in and out of the many doors and rooms. Mama Vasco, as she begged Titania to call her, seemed to enjoy the confusion. "I can never keep track of how many kids are around. We always have cousins visiting from Kauai or Maui and they bring friends, too. As long as there is plenty of room and plenty to eat, I'm happy to have 'em. And Henry just puts 'em all to work. You must make this your second home," she told Titania. "We never lock a door here. Everybody just comes and goes. You want to stay the night? We find you a bed. And if there're no beds left, we find you a couch or a hammock. Many's the morning I'd go out to feed the chickens and find Acheson or Kimo stretched out sound asleep in the hammocks. This crazy kid . . ."—she gave Acheson's cheek a motherly pinch—"he used to swear he slept better in a hammock than in a bed."

"I still do." He gave her an affectionate kiss on the cheek. "But I always slept best anywhere at Mama Vasco's." Titania found herself strangely moved at seeing this tender affection between them.

"Acheson, you gonna take your pretty friend on a tour of the ranch before dinner? After that it will be too dark. Kimo, honey, go help papa get the barbecue going."

Acheson was proud of the orchards and vegetable

fields. "Since Henry Vasco took over, we're producing everything we need for the hotel. I import very little in the way of fresh fruit and vegetables. We have fresh fish and our own cattle and chickens."

"It's no wonder the food is so delicious," she marveled. "Do you export much?"

He shook his head. "We could. Henry is always after me to expand the ranch, but I'm not interested in producing any more than exactly what is needed to support the hotel. When I mortgaged the island, I had to decide whether to invest in tourism or farm produce. The bank informed me tourism was the only enterprise they'd back. Agriculture's a bit risky on an island that doesn't have a very good water supply."

Something in what he said stood out in her mind. "You had to mortgage the entire island of Naupaka to build your resort?"

He nodded.

"But why did you have to do anything? Why not just live here and run the ranch?"

He shrugged. "Why did you open a store in Beverly Hills? Why did Maui harness the sun?"

There was a barbecue going when they returned. Mama Vasco had marinated some meat overnight and put it on skewers with tiny white onions and pineapple. "It's teriyaki," she told Titania. "I make it a lot here, leave it in the refrigerator. This way the kids can come out when they want and cook it themselves. They love that. With this many people it's almost impossible to get everybody sitting around a table at the same time."

Kimo was sitting on a hammock strumming a ukulele, to the delight of some of the younger children, making up nonsensical verses as he went along, sending them into peals of laughter.

Mama Vasco went back into the kitchen for more

meat and came out of the house with a seventeen-year-old girl in tow. "It won't hurt you to *talk* to her, Dana, come on."

"No, grandma. Not here! I'll go see her at the store. Here, she might feel *obligated*."

When the girl saw Acheson and Titania, she hung back with embarrassment, but Mama Vasco plunged ahead. "Titania, this is my granddaughter, Dana. She's crazy about clothes. Spends half her time at the sewing machine, sends away for patterns, has a subscription to *Vogue* magazine. I don't know where she gets it. Around here the kids are either in bathing suits or muu-muus. She's just graduated from high school and I thought she ought to talk to you about a job."

"Jeez, grandma," said Dana, dying of embarrassment.

"Well, it's a good age to learn the business if you're interested," said Titania good-naturedly. "And I've got to hire and train some salesgirls. Have you ever done any modeling?"

"*Modeling?* Wow, no. I wouldn't know how to stand or walk or *any*thing."

Titania appraised her. She was a tall slender girl with high cheekbones and long shiny, straight black hair. Mama Vasco was right. The girl was a natural clothes-horse. "You can work in the store, and I'll teach you how to model. If Acheson agrees, I'd like to send you around to the tables on the veranda and by the pool during lunch."

"Oh, Acheson, you'll let me, won't you?" she begged him.

He rubbed his chin, pretending to think it over. "I don't know, Dana. People might not want to have their meal disturbed."

"There's nothing women enjoy so much as a free fashion show," Titania added.

"Well, if Titania says so." He smiled.

"Acheson, you're all *right*!" exclaimed Dana. "All my life I've always wanted to do something with pretty clothes—but over here on Naupaka there wasn't much chance. I went over to Honolulu once to look for a job, but so many people and so many cars, the big high buildings—I couldn't wait to get home. Did you model? Is that how you started in the business?"

Titania noted that Dana had a charming, animated way of speaking and seemed to have inherited all her grandmother's gracious warmth. She would be easy to train as a salesgirl. "I've done a little modeling and run hundreds of fashion shows," she told the girl. "I started out at a huge department store in Los Angeles. One minute I'd be working in the lingerie department and the next I'd be selling perfume. Eventually they made me a buyer and then I had my own store."

"I don't know anything about selling," Dana admitted. "Is it very hard?"

"It's like anything else. You have to know what to do. I'll work with you at first. It won't take you long to pick it up. You're a bright girl."

Acheson seemed to be very pleased at the way Titania was fitting into the Vasco family. Out of the corner of her eye she saw Kimo look up from his ukulele and give Acheson a wink.

After dinner, Acheson, Kimo, and some of the kids went down to the huge lawn below to play softball. Titania stayed back on the veranda to watch and talk to Mama Vasco.

"We don't see Acheson over here nearly as much as we used to," she sighed. "There was a time when he was like one of my own kids. He still calls me Mama Vasco," she chuckled. "I'll never forget the day my husband brought him home. You remember that, honey?"

Mr. Vasco nodded slowly. "Poor kid, just wandering in the sugar cane fields, miles from the hotel. Couldn't have been more than five or six years old. Heaven only knows how he got there."

"You never saw such a sad little face in your life." Mama Vasco shook her head. "Looked like a little menehune, brown as a kukui berry from head to toe, part dirt and part tan, with that yellow hair like the inside of a pineapple falling down over those big blue eyes. And so thin! I took him into the kitchen and fed him. He ate like he hadn't had a crumb for a week. I couldn't believe he was the son of the Lanes."

"But didn't they have anybody to look after him?" asked Titania.

"Nah, they never cared where he went, what he did. Never once did I ever see those people sober. Every time Henry'd make a profit at the ranch, sure as anything, they'd drink it away. Little Acheson kept wandering down here so often, finally I'd just call and say he was here, keep him here for weeks. They never called or came by to pick him up."

"But didn't he miss his parents . . . I'd think a child that young . . ." Titania was thinking of her own miserable childhood, how much she had missed having a father and mother. Grandparents were never more than a substitute. There was always the hidden feeling that her own parents, if they'd stayed together, would have loved her more, treated her with more tenderness.

"Acheson hardly knew his own parents," said Mama Vasco. "And one time when I tried to take him back home he went to hide in the fields. But I thought to myself, this isn't my child—I can't keep him here forever. I found him and took him back up to the hotel. His mother was sitting in the bar, as usual. She looked at him like he was a stranger, then she told him to come to her. I had to give him a little push. Then she looked him up and down and told him to button his shirt. That's all."

"No hug or kiss even?" Titania was shocked.

"That woman? Hadn't seen her kid for three weeks and she couldn't be bothered to give him a hug or kiss. 'What a sloppy little boy you are, Acheson,' she says to him. I could have killed her. So he says, 'Mother, may I go back to Kimo's house?' See, he and Kimo were best friends. But his mother said, 'My deah, you're far too much trouble for Mrs. Vasco. Heaven knows, you're far too much trouble for me.' 'He's no trouble at all, Mrs. Lane,' I told her. 'He can stay at my house for as long as he wants.'"

"How lucky he was to have you!" said Titania, her heart aching for the little boy Acheson once was.

"Well, we love him. He and Kimo are closer than brothers, like two peas in a pod. They'd take the horses and be gone for days, camping out up in the hills. I used to worry, but papa, he say, 'They'll be okay.' He taught 'em how to get along. But you see, I'm part Hawaiian. I still remember all the stories about the menehunes of Naupaka. Papa'd say, 'No menehunes gonna bother those two. They look like menehunes. And menehunes never hurt kids. Kids and lovers.'"

Titania watched the game of softball. Acheson was behind home plate, patiently helping one of the little boys with his swing. She was seeing him for the first time in an entirely different light. It was hard to believe that this strong man brimming with self-confidence was once a little lost child wandering alone in the sugar cane fields. If he'd put his mind to seducing her, she thought, he couldn't have planned a more effective way. She could resist the sensuous lure of a roomful of tiki gods, but bringing her home to this warm family and a ranch house full of love was quite another story.

When the softball game was over, they all headed back up to the veranda. Acheson was grinning as he sat down next to her. "How're you doing, princess?"

It was the first time he'd called her that since their night of love. She looked up at him with startled eyes. The way she was feeling about him that moment, the look in his dark blue eyes—how easy it would be to resume their affair, but she held herself in check.

"The Vascos do have a wonderful way of making a visitor feel at home," she said.

He nodded. "But you must not consider yourself a visitor anymore. We're all strictly family."

"How about some coconut cookies?" Mama Vasco interrupted them with a big platter of freshly baked cookies.

"Thank you, but I don't think I could eat another thing." She laughed.

"But you're so skinny! Don't you think she's too skinny, Acheson?"

He gave her a long appraising glance and placed his hands around her tiny waist. "You're right, as usual, Mama Vasco. A trifle too thin around the middle." He lifted her easily into the air. "Put about ten more pounds on her and I might consider marrying her, if the dowry's sufficient."

Titania laughed at his teasing joke, but secretly it rankled her. He threw the word "marriage" around so easily now—had she taken him too seriously that night?

chapter 12

AFTER THAT BRIEF joking reference to marriage at the Vascos, he never mentioned it again and treated her as he would a friend and associate. Over the next few weeks she dined often with him, but it was always in the formal dining room and often in the company of other people. If she had business to discuss with him, they met in his office.

She marveled at how he seemed to be everywhere at once. One minute he was hiking across the construction site, and the next he was conferring with the chef in the kitchen or consulting with Kimo at the main desk. Often he simply chatted with guests by the pool as though he had nothing better to do with his time than pamper them with his concern.

He was often invited to join guests for dinner or to attend their private cocktail parties, and he always seemed to have time for them. She was fascinated to see how he could listen with rapt attention to the most boring of conversations and compliment even the plainest of women into feeling like a beauty. She admired the brilliant way he handled flirtatious attacks from sophisticated women. Affecting a boyish grin, he appeared to be surprised and flattered by the attention, then always found a pretext to get away. Running a resort provided him with a hundred legitimate excuses.

After observing him for several weeks, Titania began to suspect that the wild stories she had heard from Mrs. Baldwin and others were pure fantasy. Acheson Lane was simply too busy at his job to have the time to carry on amorous intrigues with his guests. They must have been suffering from an epidemic of acute wishful thinking.

Titania had not seen Karin Baldwin since that morning at the Naupaka airstrip. Jeremy mentioned that she had been into the Beverly Hills store several times and he had also told her about a lavish party he had attended at the Baldwin home. For all that Karin claimed to own Acheson Lane, he did not mention her at all. Titania, with her penchant for gossip, was curious to know exactly what was between Acheson and Karin Baldwin, but even Jeremy seemed unable to provide her with details.

It occurred to her that she could simply ask Acheson directly, but each time she began to speak of it, the words dried up in her throat. Finally she realized that she really did not *want* to hear anything about Karin Baldwin.

Acheson was taking great interest in the store, dropping in unexpectedly several times throughout the day. "I'm going to need some shelves put in over here," she told him one morning. "It will be an excellent place for the sandals, good natural light from the window to show them off."

"You're going to stock shoes?" he asked with surprise.

"Just a few sandals," she said. "Before I left Beverly Hills, I had a long talk with the owner of the Casual Aire stores in Honolulu. All her shops are in hotels and she says you absolutely have to stock items like sandals, slips, a few nightgowns. Somebody always forgets to pack things like that in a suitcase."

"You've done your homework." He seemed pleased at her attention to those details. "I'll send a carpenter over to put in the shelves you need. How did you like the lighting I had installed for the dressing rooms?"

"Horrible."

"But you wanted fluorescent fixtures," he protested.

"Not with that ghastly blue tint. They'll reveal wrinkles our poor customers don't even know they have. There's a natural fluorescent you can get; it shows off the clothes, but it's much softer. By the way, Dana Vasco is a darling."

"I'm glad to hear that. Mama Vasco will be pleased. All the Vascos were crazy about you, especially mama. They'd love to have you drop over there anytime."

Dana, of course, had told her much the same thing, but hearing it from Acheson gave her a pleasant warmth. "I've been meaning to, but with the store so close to opening, I've been here every night. I'd forgotten how many details there are to attend to: ticketing the clothes, ordering the bags, getting all the credit card accounts set up."

"Hey, even the Bible says you have to take off one day a week. What do you say to a picnic Sunday?"

"Just the two of us?" Her pulse was racing, but she tried to appear calm.

"Are you afraid of me or afraid of yourself?" He grinned mischievously at her.

"I'm afraid of the menehunes," she shot back sarcastically.

He laughed. "I'll pack the picnic basket full of treats for them. Besides, it's time you had a tour of Naupaka. So far you've only seen the hotel and the ranch. The real beauty of the place is up in the mountains."

It was an appeal she found difficult to resist. "Well, as long as you promise to behave."

"Don't I always?" He gave her a brilliant smile that made her knees feel weak.

She had discovered at Naupaka that one really needed very few clothes for leisure time. Just as Mama Vasco had said, a bathing suit and a muu-muu sufficed for almost every occasion. Luckily the customers staying at the hotel would feel the need to be more stylishly clothed; otherwise, she would be out of business. That morning Titania wore a bikini and, over it, a comfortable, loose-fitting cotton shirt.

Acheson had on a faded-blue tee shirt and threadbare swim trunks. "If I didn't know you, I'd still think you were the nineteen-year-old lifeguard," she teased him.

"My days off are few and far between. My 'more-genteel-than-thou' image also needs a day off now and then. Sometimes I think Kimo has the right idea. For him work is secondary. Enjoying life is first."

In a few minutes they were beyond the hotel grounds and the dirt road became bumpier winding up through the emerald-green hills.

"This scenery!" She gazed around her, eyes wide, taking it all in. The road was partially overgrown with thick ferns and taro plants. Above them were stark, craggy green cliffs sweeping majestically up to the cobalt blue sky. "Everything seems to glow here," she said with wonder. "At home the hills are kind of a dusty olive-brown most of the year, but I guess the moisture and the rainfall here keep everything looking like springtime."

As they rounded a turn, he stopped the jeep and pointed across the road. A stream of blue water was cascading down several thousand feet into the gorge below. "When the winds are right, the water sprays back up from the valley. Kimo and I used to call it the Upside-down Falls. We were sure the menehunes made it do that."

The road became increasingly rutted. Acheson steered the jeep skillfully, avoiding the overhanging branches of the gnarled kukui trees, but finally the road became too narrow to go any farther and Acheson pulled over to the side. "It's not far now. We can hike in. He hoisted a Styrofoam cooler onto his broad shoulders and handed her some towels and rolled-up grass mats.

With the jeep motor off, she began to hear the sounds of the jungle that surrounded them—the cawing of exotic birds, the clicks of insects. She could not see the path, but Acheson knew the way. Though barefoot, he was totally unconcerned where he stepped.

Several times he had to hold overhanging branches aside for her. The delicate white ginger flowers she admired grew in abundance here, along with the Naupaka and its strange half blossoms. There were ohia lehua trees with red flowers, which from a distance looked like so many Christmas ornaments but up close were feathery soft with spindly petals. "These are used to make leis for Pele, the volcano goddess," explained Acheson. "The ohia lehua is sacred to her."

A light warm rain began to fall on them, and she asked, "Do you think we'll have a storm?"

"No, it rains like this all the time in the mountains. You'll appreciate it later on in the afternoon when the sun is at its peak."

They were following a stream, sometimes crossing it when the branches of the bamboo shoots became too thick for them to stay on the path. The sound of splashing water was growing louder. Titania, who had been looking down to watch her footing, glanced up and drew in her breath.

Before them was a natural pool surrounded by ferns and smooth black volcanic rocks. Water was cascading down from a cliff above, making several stops among the boulders and finally fanning out over a wide smooth rock and splashing into a green pool below. Flowers grew close to the water's edge, bushes of red and yellow-orange Hibiscus and bird-of-paradise flowers in beds of white Naupaka and ginger. There were even wild purple orchids hidden between the ferns and the glistening red, heart-shaped Anthuriums.

Titania could not speak for a moment as the dazzling sight overwhelmed her.

Acheson set the cooler among the foliage near the water and spread out the grass mats for them. "The moss that grows here makes a wonderfully comfortable bed," he told her.

"Don't get any ideas," she warned him jokingly.

"I was just being informative." He smiled. "In fact, they used to ship the moss to China to stuff mattresses and pillows."

He took off his shirt and lay back, closing his eyes to the sun's rays. It was ten o'clock already and the sunbeams pouring onto the pool were warming even its shady recesses. Stretched out on his grass mat, surrounded by the green moss, his blond hair flowing out behind his head and light chest hair curling down over his abdomen, Acheson looked like the sea god caressed by the rays of sunlight that seemed to delight in painting his powerful body golden brown.

She decided first to shed her cotton shirt and take a swim. Thinking the water would be cool, she hesitated before plunging in, but it was as warm as the ocean around the island, and she slid into it easily.

Floating serenely on her back, she watched the blue-tinged clouds move across the sky and then swam close to the waterfall, laughing as the shower bathed her. Acheson, who had been watching her, suddenly dove into the pool and swam toward her. "Come on, let me show you where the menehunes live. It's time you met them."

Hidden behind the waterfall, to her surprise, were some low caves. He ducked under the ferns that hung down like green necklaces, and she followed. It was cooler in the grotto, and easy to lose their footing on the slippery pebbles as they waded through. The walls of the cave became narrower, pungent with the cold smell of damp moss. She felt a chill as a cool breeze caught the beads of water on her arms.

"Kimo and I discovered this place as kids," he said. "I don't think anyone'd ever been up here before."

"Except the menehunes, of course," she corrected him.

He helped her over some jagged black volcanic rocks. The forest was thick with bamboo and heavy green foliage so dark that it was almost like night. Only narrow ribbons of sunlight filtered through. "You see?" He was pointing to a stone ledge. As they neared it, she could see that small stones had been fitted together tightly. It had obviously been constructed, not formed naturally. They followed the stone ledge until they came to another cave.

Inside, drawings had been carved on the smooth surface of the volcanic rock. "Menehunes are great builders and great doodlers," he joked. "Imagine what they could do with spray cans."

Some of the images were easy to recognize—human stick figures, some with their hair sticking straight up, some fishing. There were canoes and animals, but most of the scratches were impossible to decipher. "Have you ever brought an anthropologist up here to unravel this?" she asked with fascination.

"Petroglyphs like these are found all over the Hawaiian Islands. I don't know if anyone would be interested in these."

"And you're sure they're done by menehunes?" She gave him a suspicious smile.

He laughed. "Why not?"

"Well, where *are* these little people? You said you were going to introduce me."

"They're watching us," he teased. "But they only

come out at night, and they rarely show themselves to humans."

She looked around her. The place was certainly strange and the petroglyphs were close enough to the ground to have been done by elves. It gave her an eerie feeling on the back of her neck. "Have *you* ever seen them?"

"Kimo and I came up here one night. We must have been about ten. It took all day to get here on horseback. We heard some strange noises in the night and, of course, with the imaginations of children, we were sure they were ghosts and spirits. We called to them and asked them to make themselves visible to us, but they never appeared. I keep telling myself that some day I'm going to come back up here again at night and try to make contact, but there never seems to be the time."

"You're the weirdest person." She laughed. "I think you really do believe they're here."

They walked out into the sunlight, and he plucked a yellow Hibiscus and put it in her hair, brushing her smooth cheek with the tip of his finger. "Have you never felt that chill on the back of your neck, Titania—when people are talking about otherwordly things."

"Well, yes," she admitted reluctantly, "I did back there."

"The ancient Celtic poets used to say that was proof of their existence."

True or not, she felt the enchantment of the cave, the towering green cliffs, and the thick tropical jungle, but her turbulent feelings seemed due more to the presence of Acheson Lane than the presence of elves. It would take all her earthly power to resist him, if he decided he wanted her again.

The chef had packed mangoes and papayas, fresh pineapples, cold chicken, and sparkling white wine that was chilled from the ice. They spread out the feast on a small, fine linen tablecloth and made a toast, "To the menehunes," clinking the crystal glasses. The delicious food, the wine, and the heat of midday were all combined with the effects of the vigorous hike through the jungle. They stretched out lazily on the grass mats in the sun.

Titania reached for her bottle of coconut oil that Dana had assured her produced the best tropical tan and applied it to her legs. "Would you like me to rub some on your back?" Acheson asked her.

She looked at him suspiciously, but a little oil certainly was not a compromise. She lay down on her stomach while he spread the oil, his large hand spanning the width of her small waist. She unhooked the top to her bikini so he wouldn't get oil on it and also so that she wouldn't have a white line when she wore backless dresses.

"Your muscles are tense," he informed her as he lifted the long hair off the back of her neck, "all knotted up here." His strong fingers began kneading the unyielding knots in her shoulders and she flinched at the shooting pain. "This comes from working too hard. I know it hurts, but this is the only way to relax them."

She could feel the tension leaving as he massaged, moving his hands down across the taut muscles of her shoulders and spine. She was drifting into a lazy euphoria, enjoying giving herself over to his hands and the warmth of the sun, the rippling splashes of water cascading over the falls.

"There," he said, putting the cap on the bottle and leaning back on his own mat. "Feel better?"

"It was feeling wonderful; I hate to have you stop," she said dreamily.

"Then I won't." He twisted the cap back off the bottle. "I'll work on your legs."

Before she could protest, he was rubbing the balls of

her feet, her toes, and ankles. Those muscles and ten-
dons, too, had tightened from the hike through the forest
and now loosened under his expert touch. Moving his
hands slowly, he pressed the calves of her legs. Titania
let herself float, entrusting her body to him. She had
never allowed herself the luxury of a professional massage, and she was beginning to understand now why her
customers claimed to spend a fortune on them. Carefully
he awakened each nerve ending, making it tingle with
pleasure. Somewhere in the back of her mind, she knew
that this might turn into a preliminary for lovemaking,
but she put it out of her mind. For the moment, she was
the center of the universe; her own sensations—not the
store, not the personal problems with Jeremy—were all
that mattered. Never before in her life had Titania felt
so pampered, so much like a fairy princess.

"Come on." He rolled her gently over. "Now I'll get
the other half of you."

She squinted and smiled up at him. "All this work
must be awfully tedious for you."

"Yes. You're lucky I'm such a good sport." He massaged her arms, her graceful fingers, and as he came
back up to her shoulders he pulled her bikini top in place.
"Rest assured, your modesty is secure with me, madam."

"You are behaving admirably," she murmured, eyes
closed. She almost wished he wasn't, for in spite of his
avoidance of the erotic areas, she was alarmingly
aroused. Everywhere his hands kneaded and caressed
seemed touched by a magic wand. He was pressing his
strong thumbs into the soft flesh of her inner thighs,
circling round and round. She was beginning to breathe
with difficulty, her lips parted, and, as she opened one
eye, she saw that he had placed himself between her legs
and was watching her face as he worked. He smiled

lazily at her and continued, this time with a lighter touch than before, moving tantalizingly closer to the edge of her bikini. One hand circled her belly, the other her thigh. This was no longer a massage. It was provocation and she was growing increasingly aware of her desire for more.

"Acheson," she whispered. Her mouth was dry. How she needed his lips to quench the unbearable thirst.

His thumbs were pressing into the soft flesh below her ribs, circling, rubbing. Her back was arching to him in spite of her efforts to maintain control.

"Acheson, I . . ."

He kneeled over her and brushed his lips across her belly.

"No, Acheson . . ."

He gave a throaty laugh and ignored her. She reached out to push him away but caught only the wild mane of his thick hair as he bent over her. By then it was too late to protest.

Her mind raced along the valleys and gorges of the tropical jungles and elfin caves hidden behind thick primeval ferns. Her legs wrapped around his back like the clinging violet morning glories that twisted around the kukui trees.

His lips were caressing hers, whispering "Titania" as though it were the sound of a breeze rustling through the palm fronds. Her fingers flitted through his thick golden mane and across his strong shoulders, grasping his massive back as though he were a verdant cliff jutting out to the sky and she were in danger of falling, plunging like a waterfall from its dizzying heights.

They rolled off the mats in the soft, damp moss, sinking into each other, making their oneness with the fragrant earth and velvety flowers, tasting the flavor of the salt air on their smooth skin.

"Perhaps we should stay here tonight and greet the menehunes," she whispered as he held her afterward in his strong arms.

"We could—that is, if you're not afraid." He kissed her forehead.

She covered the palm of his hand with kisses. "How could I be afraid? Mama Vasco said the menehunes protect children and lovers."

They dozed off under the shade of a giant kukui tree and awoke gradually as the afternoon began to cool, then made love again as they bathed in the warm shallow water of the pool. "You're the most beautiful woman in the world," he told her as she floated on her back, her long honey-colored hair fanning out behind her on the water.

It occurred to her how odd the word "beautiful" sounded. She had been called "pretty" as a girl, "stylish," a "fashionable young woman," but never "beautiful." Now she knew that she was, without the aid of cosmetics and expensive designer clothes. It came from within, from the happiness she felt with Acheson.

There was still plenty of food left from lunch and another bottle of wine. Acheson picked some fresh mangoes from a nearby tree. As night fell, the reflecting water turned dark green, then black. The forest took on new sounds and the air, already full of moisture, wrapped around them like a damp cloak.

A half-moon gave scant light through the overhanging leaves and branches, and the heady fragrances of the tropical flowers became more pungent as the sky filled with stars. Titania lay back dreamily in his arms. "I'm still waiting for them. Where are your little creatures?"

"They should be here." He feigned concern. "I sent out the invitations months ago."

"What sort of occasion did you say it was going to be?"

"A wedding, of course."

"Oh?" She tried to laugh, but the word "wedding" disturbed her too much, reminding her of another wedding.

"You didn't get your invitation?" He turned her face to him. "I'll have my secretary fired."

He forced her to look into his eyes. "The Fairy Princess Titania, methinks, is about to jump up and run out into yon forest."

"Methinks thou art perceptive, handsome knave." She gave a nervous laugh.

He grew serious. "Titania, I've been waiting half my life for you, dreaming of you. I came to this very place a few years ago, before I even knew you'd be back in my life—and I imagined making love to you here. We will be married, my love."

"Acheson, marriage is . . . well, it's more than making love in a tropical rain forest protected from reality by the menehunes. Even Adam and Eve woke up when they left the Garden of Eden."

"Titania, just because you made one bad choice doesn't mean that marriage is bad." He lifted a strand of her long hair and twirled it in his fingers.

"You don't understand," she sighed with exasperation. "I thought I'd made a good choice the first time. I was in love, *very* much in love. Jeremy was. . ." In saying his name, her voice began to crack. Lying there naked with another man still seemed to her like a betrayal to the man she had once sworn to love forever.

There was no denying the strong feelings for Acheson—but was it love she felt? How could you love two men?

Acheson's mouth hardened and his blue eyes gleamed black with anger in the darkness. "I keep forgetting you're still in love with him. It's not hard to do when you make love to me. Why did you divorce Jeremy if you still love him?" His voice was rough-edged, like the jagged volcanic rocks.

"Jeremy didn't want a divorce. He still doesn't. He thought we could go on in a kind of 'open marriage,' with him having mistresses."

"And *you* having lovers?"

"Yes, but I didn't want lovers and I didn't want him to have mistresses either. If I couldn't satisfy him . . ." She was aware now of the tears filling her eyes. "Acheson, you might get bored with me, too. Did you think about that? I wonder if I could hold any man's interest for very long."

"Your husband was a blithering idiot," he said harshly. "You're more woman than any man could ever hope to hold in his arms." He wiped the tears from her cheeks with the tips of his long fingers and pulled her head onto his chest, smoothing out the long, silky hair.

"And you feel nothing for me?" he asked tightly.

She pulled away to look at his chiseled features, the thick golden hair. He reached up and rubbed the back of his fingers across her smooth cheek. "Acheson, I do feel something for you—the minute you walk into a room. Do you remember those old Disney movies when the magic wand was waved and you saw zillions of tiny twinkling stars?—well, that's how you make me feel. But I'm not sure that's love."

"Of course it is!" He pulled her back down to him and held her trembling body against him.

"Maybe it's love," she admitted reluctantly.

"What else could it be?"

"I don't know. Some sort of sexual attraction, perhaps."

Suddenly he looked at her with knowing eyes. "Then what you feel for me is not what you feel for your ex-husband?"

"No, it isn't," she said in a voice barely audible.

"When *he* walks into a room," Acheson prodded her, "how do you feel?"

"A sort of rage fills me up."

"But not the zillions of twinkling stars?"

"Not at all. What are you getting at?"

He kissed her lightly. "Princess, did it ever occur to you that what you feel toward him *is* rage, not love?"

"But . . ." She had lived so long with the certainty that her reaction to Jeremy was love that this idea left her speechless.

"Titania," he murmured softly, "I don't expect you to understand all at once, but you will. And I'm going to marry you. On this very spot. We have witnesses. Do you hear me, menehunes?" he said loudly in the direction of the caves.

Out of the darkness, through the night sounds that were now becoming familiar, came the sound of footsteps padding softly across the moss-covered ground.

Acheson tensed and whispered, "Don't make a sound," but she could not have spoken a word if she tried. An eerie chill raised the hackles on the back of her neck, and she clung to Acheson tightly.

chapter 13

ACHESON GAVE A low whistle that sounded like the cooing of an exotic bird, and somehow Titania was not at all surprised to find him capable of such an animal sound. After a moment, the cooing was returned and the footsteps continued toward them. He tossed a towel to her and reached for her bikini and told her to put it on; but without bothering to cover himself, he stood up.

She put the bikini on quickly. "You're not going to leave me, are you?" she asked in the high frightened voice of a child.

"Of course not." He laughed. "It's only Kimo."

She let the compressed air out of her lungs with a relieved laugh. "Kimo? Why didn't you tell me?"

"You didn't really think it was the menehunes? My lady of the rational world? No such thing as elves?" She could see Kimo emerge from the shadows as Acheson went toward him.

The sound of their voices was partially muffled by the cascading falls and the trade winds blowing away from her. What she could make out was that there was some trouble at the hotel that Kimo could not handle. "I didn't want to bother you up here," Kimo apologized to his friend as they walked toward her. "Here's the first day you take off in months, and you can't even be alone to enjoy it. Hi, Titania."

Acheson slipped his arm around her. "Kimo's going to drive you back down to the hotel. I've got to get there in a hurry and the way I drive these roads, you'd have cardiac arrest."

"Be careful—the cliffs and the ruts..." she began. She was thinking of his parents' tragic death but didn't want to say it.

"Acheson could drive these roads blindfolded," said Kimo reassuringly. "We were up and down here so often as kids. The two us us cut this road up here. Believe me, we know every inch."

"What's the problem at the hotel?" she asked as she gathered her things. There was a brief silence, and she saw Kimo and Acheson exchange a glance.

"One of the guests...just arrived...room she wanted not available...causing a ruckus," said Kimo quickly, running the words together. Acheson shot him a grateful glance that Titania, sensitive as she was, did not fail to catch. It was clear she was not being told everything.

Acheson kissed her for a long, lingering moment that held in it all the memories of the afternoon and evening, then hurried down the dark path. In a moment he was swallowed up by the rain forest.

Kimo was a bit awkward. "Here, I've got a flashlight. It will be easier to see the path." They made their way carefully, and by the time they reached the road where Acheson had parked, he had already gone. She settled into Kimo's jeep and he drove cautiously along the dirt road. She could not help but be suspicious that he was driving a bit too cautiously, even to protect her. Was there a reason he was going so slowly? Was there something or someone she was not supposed to see at the hotel?

"That must have been quite an emergency for you to come all the way up here this late at night."

"It's not really that late." He picked up on the last part of the question, she realized, to avoid the first. "Seems like it's late when you're up here. Couldn't be more than about nine o'clock. Funny, how time passes in a tropical forest. Did Acheson take you to see the Menehune Caves?"

Whatever it was that Kimo was concealing, Titania knew that no amount of prying was going to get it out of Acheson's best friend.

She gave up and let the conversation drift comfortably around the legends and some boyhood stories.

"You get up near the Menehune Caves or out in the ocean—where there's sky above you and air and flowers—and after a while you *need* it, you can't live any other way. That's why you don't see too many Hawaiians on the mainland. This kind of life becomes a part of you. Acheson's got this bug about the hotel but still sneaks off here, see? It's in him and eventually it's got to come out."

Looking over the sides of cliffs, she began to see the ocean below, the waves sparkling white against the black sea in the moonlight. Far below from time to time she could see the headlights of Acheson's jeep as it careened at breakneck speed down the mountain.

"The hotel means a great deal to him, doesn't it, Kimo?"

"It's beyond me." He shook his head. "After his parents died and we graduated from the University of Hawaii, he had no interest in it at all. We'd work hard in the fields all week with my dad, then take off in my rickety old Cessna for Honolulu and party all weekend. It was a good life," he mused nostalgically.

"Then what changed him?" she asked with growing curiosity.

Kimo drove along thoughtfully for a few minutes.

"It was the crowd we got into in Honolulu. A fast crowd, lots of money. The Baldwins from Beverly Hills were at one party. I couldn't believe it. This gorgeous wahine and this old dude. She took one look at Acheson and decided she had to have him. I don't even think her husband knew—or cared—what was going on. Seemed to me she was just like an ornament to him, another expensive toy. She was taking off for this resort hotel in Bali while the old man went back to his bank on the mainland, and she invited Acheson to go with her."

Kimo laughed as he remembered. "Three weeks later I get a phone call. 'Kimo man,' he says, 'Get on an airplane and come on over here. I'm at the Bali Oberoi Hotel. I'm the assistant general manager and you're assistant to the assistant general manager.' Sounded less back-breaking than harvesting sugar cane, so I went."

Titania shook her head. "How in the world did he get that job?"

"You know Acheson. He can talk anybody into anything. Made them think he'd run Naupaka single-handedly. But you should see this hotel on Bali, it's even got outdoor bathrooms."

"That sounds to me like a step backward," teased Titania.

"No, you'd have to see these bathrooms, like gardens—tiled bathtub-jacuzzis. Each villa with its own swimming pool. Acheson said to me, 'Learn everything you can because this is the most luxurious hotel in the world—and exactly what we're gonna do on Naupaka. Only it's going to be better.'"

"And all this time Mrs. Baldwin was there on Bali with you?"

Kimo shrugged. "No, she was back in Beverly Hills. Acheson had that all planned, too. Somebody had to put up the money for this expensive scheme of his."

Titania's mouth fell open. "Then the Baldwin Bank is underwriting Naupaka?"

Kimo nodded.

Titania remembered what Karin Baldwin had said that day at the Naupaka airstrip. No wonder she had been so sure of herself. Acheson was tied to her with purse strings.

"You should have seen this place the day we re-opened," Kimo continued. "Acheson spent a fortune promoting the place. Brought forty-three travel agents over from the mainland, all expenses paid."

"Good publicity for him," commented Titania.

"Yeah, but this old hotel was in such bad shape it had taken us six months just to get it together, and even then the plumbing men were still working on getting the toilets to flush. Acheson and I were so worried about the crunchy wiring, the peeling paint, the cracks in the pool that we forgot one thing. We got forty-three travel agents arriving the next day and we haven't got one single mattress."

"What in the world did you do?"

"Well, Acheson and I are standing there in the lobby greeting these forty-three hot and tired travel agents when this occurs to us. So he says, 'Kimo-man, take them all out on the golf course and get 'em drunk while I figure out something.'"

"Couldn't he call Honolulu and have some shipped over from a mattress company?"

"He already had 'em on order, but it was Saturday. So when he calls the mattress company, everybody had gone to the beach. Nobody knows anything about our order. Finally Acheson gets a guy who says they're at air cargo at the airport. We can pick 'em up, he says, if we come get 'em.

"Meanwhile, all forty-three travel agents are sprawled out on the golf course. I say to Acheson, 'Why not let 'em sleep out there?'

"Finally, I called Honolulu and got hold of a Twin Otter. I flew over there in my Cessna with a couple kids from the ranch. We stuffed forty-three mattresses in the Otter and got back just before dark. What a day!"

"And the people weren't angry at the delay?"

"Nah! People don't get mad at Acheson. He has a way with them. I've never seen anything like it. Like tonight when . . ." He stopped himself before he realized.

"I hope he got everything straightened out," she pressed him.

"I'm sure he did," said Kimo with a nervous laugh. "Hey, we're almost back to the hotel. Would you mind if we took a little detour by the ranch? I've got to pick up some things. I know mama would love to see you."

She knew he was putting her off longer, but she played along. It would do little good to protest. Besides, it would be pleasant to see the Vascos again.

Mama Vasco welcomed her with open arms. "I'm so glad to see you! Our little Dana is in seventh heaven at your store. How nice you are to take so much time with her."

"I enjoy her, Mama Vasco. She's a wonderful girl."

While it was fun to chat with Mama Vasco and Dana, who had joined them on the lanai, she began to wonder what was taking Kimo so long. It had already been over an hour.

Finally, he appeared with a mumbled apology and a feeble excuse about not being able to find what he needed, and they drove back to the hotel.

As soon as they arrived, she started toward the main building, but Kimo tried to steer her to her bungalow.

She broke away from him. "I see Acheson's light on," she said, testing Kimo. "I'll go on up to his suite and see how he's doing."

"Uh, Titania, why don't you go on to your bungalow and I'll tell him you're back." He put a warning hand on her arm.

"Okay, Kimo." She gazed at him directly. "What's the big secret?"

"No secret." He avoided her eyes. "Just that it's probably better to wait for him to call you. That's just the way Acheson is."

"Well, if you're not going to tell me, I'll have to find out for myself." She went quickly up the stairs of the veranda and into the hotel lobby.

Kimo was right behind her. "Uh, Titania, maybe you could..."

She stopped abruptly in front of the bell captain's desk. There was an expensive set of dark-blue suede luggage that belonged, Titania knew, to only one person. She herself had gone to Neiman-Marcus and picked it out to match a suede coat for Mrs. Karin Baldwin.

chapter 14

KIMO'S WORDS FLOATED back to her. *One of the guests...just arrived...room she wanted not available...causing a ruckus...*The room she wanted—Acheson's penthouse suite? Obviously it had been an important enough ruckus to cause Acheson to hurry back.

She stared at the pieces of luggage as though they were the forbidding Baldwin herself. Kimo saw by her expression that she knew.

"Come on, Titania," he said, "I'll walk you back to your bungalow. You can talk to Acheson later."

Titania held back her tears. "Kimo, is he in love with her? You *must* tell me." He walked alongside her quietly, reluctant to talk.

"I wish you'd wait and talk to Acheson," he said awkwardly.

Titania grabbed his arm. "Please, Kimo. Just tell me that. Is he in love with Karin Baldwin? You're his best friend; you must know."

They were standing in front of her bungalow door. Kimo took a deep breath. "This is between you and Acheson. He and I made a vow years ago not to meddle in each other's personal business."

"But Karin Baldwin?" she asked helplessly.

"The luggage you saw was downstairs in the lobby," Kimo pointed out, "not in Acheson's room."

"But he came rushing back here tonight," protested Titania, the humiliating anger mounting. What right did Acheson Lane have to propose marriage when he was ready, at the drop of a hat, to rush off to another woman? It was easy to promise an endless idyll of cascading waterfalls and wild ginger blossoms; quite another to live up to it.

"He owes her a lot," said Kimo simply. "If nothing else, an explanation."

"I see." Titania felt weak. She had grappled with the force of Karin Baldwin before and lost a husband. She hadn't won then with a marriage contract behind her and now she was up against an entire island. Acheson was mortgaged to the Baldwin Bank. No matter how much he might love her, it would always be necessary to placate Mrs. Baldwin.

Titania sank into the chaise on her lanai. Was there no escape from the patterns that wove themselves into the same designs again and again in her life? Once again it was Karin Baldwin who was turning her life into a nightmare.

The telephone inside rang and automatically Titania started toward it. But something made her stop before reaching for the receiver. It had to be Acheson, wanting to explain. It was all too clear what he would say. She had heard the same excuses from Jeremy. At least, she thought, she had learned something from the disastrous marriage.

Leaving the telephone ringing, she slipped out the door and headed toward the beach. She was still wearing her bathing suit and it was a warm night. A brisk walk on the sand and a swim would help calm her down.

The Naupaka beach stretched for miles, curving in a

semicircle and ending at the cliffs to the south and rocks to the north. On the other side of the rocks was where Acheson had taken her surfing that night long ago. The tide was in and the rocks were almost covered over with the splashing foam. She figured it would be another few hours before they were completely under water and she climbed across easily onto the other side.

Jogging in the sand, she let the tropical night air fill her lungs. The turmoil over Acheson and Mrs. Baldwin had suddenly infused her with nervous energy.

At a short distance, leaning against a palm tree, was a surfboard. Kimo's? Acheson's? She wondered if she could still remember how to surf. It had been so many years before, and even then she had hardly mastered it. Acheson had been there paddling behind her. The one time she had tried, she had fallen off balance into the waves.

Out of curiosity she went over to the board. The newer ones were light, easy to carry. The temptation was great. Perhaps she wouldn't try to surf on it but just paddle it out a short distance. She lifted it out of the sand, but it was not as light as she had imagined. It also occurred to her that she would feel terrible if it ended up smashed on the rocks. She left it leaning against the tree and walked back down to the water. A short brisk swim would settle her frayed nerves.

As she slipped into the water, she felt a tranquilizing peace flow over her like the gentle waves. Naupaka was a wondrous place—just as she had imagined it would be as a child. Acheson Lane or no Acheson Lane, she loved the island.

If only she had kept her relationship with Acheson strictly business! Jeremy had ridiculed her celibacy, but actually life was simpler without romance. People were always dying of love, but nobody ever died of indifference. In looking over her life, she decided that work was the least disappointing of anything she had ever done. It was the one thing that didn't let you down. You worked hard and were rewarded with satisfaction and money.

As she swam farther and farther out, she became more resolved. She would continue to live at Naupaka, going back to the mainland several times a year to buy. There were the charming Vascos, a beautiful beach, hiking trails to explore. It would be a good, fulfilling existence. And she would carefully isolate herself from the slings and arrows 'of amorous men.

The lights of the hotel looked very tiny and insignificant from where she tread water. It was like looking at earth from outer space. All her personal problems, from that distance, looked just as tiny and insignificant.

It was hard to judge exactly how far out she was, but suddenly she was tired and wished she had stayed closer to shore. There was no lifeguard with her now. He was probably back in his penthouse suite placating a very rich lady. Titania took a deep breath and kicked up her legs to start the swim back, but as she did, her toes scraped against something sharp—there was a sting of pain. She was no longer in deep water. There were craggy rocks below her, even as far out as she was. Vaguely she remembered something about a coral reef. With some effort, she began to swim toward shore.

The moon was very high in the sky now and cast a pale light over the ocean; the crests of the waves looked fluorescent on the black mass of the Pacific. She stretched her arms forward in swifter strokes, but exhaustion made it difficult and her skinned toes were stinging from contact with the salt water. Had they been cut deeper than she thought?

In the distance she saw what she thought was a dark sail—a catamaran out this late? No, it was closer and coming toward her. A scream held in the back of her throat as she became paralyzed with fear. With frightening certainty she realized that it was the dorsal fin of a shark attracted to the blood from the coral cut on her toes. She tried to fight the waves, but the undertow was very strong and kept pulling her out to sea. As hard as she strained her arms and legs to propel her forward, she knew she could not outrace the shark who, in his territory, had all the advantages.

A scream started in her throat, but she held it back. Who would hear it?

chapter 15

STRANGE THOUGHTS RACED through her mind. She knew she should be seeing her life flash before her, but her main concern was fighting to make it to shore. Suddenly she saw a man with gold white hair on a surfboard floating over the top of a wave and paddling toward her.

"Acheson!" Never had she been happier to see anyone. He was off the surfboard and was helping her on, climbing on behind her, paddling with his sure, powerful strokes. Remembering from the past, she imitated the rhythm of his strokes to help them gain speed.

The dorsal fin was moving steadily toward them. "Hang on!" shouted Acheson. She gripped the sides of the board as she felt them lift into the air and glide forward in the curl of the wave. She thought she saw the shark surfing the wave with them, then it mysteriously disappeared.

As soon as they hit shallow water, Acheson hurried her toward the beach. Dropping his board in the sand, he lifted her up in his arms and carried her toward the rocks.

"I'm grateful to you, lifeguard"—she smiled up at him—"but I can walk from here."

"Sure you can," he said with an angry sarcasm that shocked her. "Look at your feet!"

"Oh," she murmured when she looked down. Her toes

had been badly ripped by the coral and were bleeding.

"Got to get that cleaned out or you'll get an infection. Whatever possessed you to swim out there alone this time of night? You've got to be crazy. You could have killed yourself!"

Titania was surprised to see him in such a rage. "That shark would probably treat me with more compassion than you," she said flatly.

"The shark was the least of your worries. It was just a baby. They used to surf with me and Kimo all the time when we were kids. But you were out way too far, heading right toward that coral reef," he continued in the same deep, blasting tone. His blue eyes were shooting daggers at her. "You know the lifeguards don't allow the guests to swim out beyond the rocks."

"If it's so dangerous, how come you brought me to this beach all those years before?" she said petulantly.

"*I* was with you that night."

He carried her as if she were light as a child and started over the rocks that separated them from the hotel beach. "Acheson, let me down. You can't get over these rocks carrying me."

"You can't get over them with your feet in that condition. Let me worry about it. I've climbed over these rocks in driving storms, carrying surfboards heavier than you." The white water crashed up against them, but Acheson was as steady as a rock himself. There was nothing for Titania to do but to keep her arms around his neck and lay her head against his broad muscled chest.

She was exhausted now. The fright of the shark had drained her of energy. He set her down only when they had reached her bungalow door. "Where's your key?"

"I left it back on the beach," she apologized. He was making her feel like a naughty litte girl, and she resented it.

"Well, fortunately you left your balcony door open, in case anyone wanted to get in." He swung himself easily over the ledge, walked into the bungalow, and opened the front door for her.

Standing for only a few minutes on her injured feet was painful, but she would not let him carry her any farther. Holding him off, she walked into the bathroom and ran the water in the bathtub over her feet to wash off the blood.

"I don't suppose you have any antiseptic," he asked, frowning.

She shook her head, clenching her teeth so she wouldn't cry out from the stinging pain.

"I'll get some," he said and was out the door.

She inspected her toes more closely. There weren't many cuts, nor were they as deep as she had imagined. What a lot of trouble, she thought miserably, for a midnight swim.

Acheson reappeared in a minute with a first-aid kit. "Kimo and I used to get cut up weekly on coral. We had to try the waves at all the beaches around. His mother was always patching up one of us."

They sat on the edge of the bathtub. He spread a towel over his lap and placed her foot on it.

"Ow! That hurts!" She pulled her foot away.

"It's supposed to hurt or it doesn't do any good. If you're brave enough to face sharks at midnight, you're brave enough for this."

"What are you poking around for?" she asked testily.

"To get the coral out, or you'll get a fungus infection. I know. I've had them. Now keep still." Leaving the bathroom for a moment. He found an unopened bottle of rum in her kitchenette and poured her a glass. "Here, drink this."

She took a sip. "I've got to mix this with something." She opened her mouth wide to force some air down her burning throat.

"No. Drink it straight."

"You're trying to torture me." She frowned.

"One gulp."

"Will it kill the pain?"

"No, but if you drink it down, in a few moments you won't care." He wore a half smile. "Go on, get it down," he said more gently.

She felt better that he was warming up to her and was so grateful she obeyed him like a dutiful child. The rum took effect and she watched him wash and clean the wounds with a careless detachment. She remembered how earlier that night she had covered the palms of those same strong, skillful hands with kisses. "You should have been a doctor, not a hotel owner," she mused.

"Keep quiet. You move your toes when you talk."

"My toes could be in the other room for all I care about them at the moment."

"Well, consider yourself lucky they're not floating in some shark's belly right now."

"Acheson?"

He was wrapping gauze around her toes and did not look up. "Mmm?"

"Thank you."

Setting her feet down on the floor, he stood up and came to her, tilting her face to him. "Titania," he said softly, "I love you. Don't do anything crazy like this again. If you want to swim at night, let me know and I'll go with you."

In a rush, she remembered the Neiman-Marcus luggage in the lobby. "You were busy tonight."

His face tightened. "If you did that to punish me, you

were being very childish and stupid!" His blue eyes were blazing again. "I called as soon as I knew you were back."

She stood up with difficulty and walked back into the living room of the bungalow. Drinking straight rum so fast had made her dizzy, and she reached out to the wall for support. But Acheson was quickly beside her, holding her tightly around the waist.

"Acheson," she said wearily, "I *know* why you had to rush back." She sank down on one of the rattan chairs.

"What is it that you *think* you know?"

"I'm too tired to go into it. Let's talk about it tomorrow." Her head felt unbelievably heavy. As her eyelids closed, she saw the rolling waves tossing her up and down.

In a swift movement, just as he had lifted her out of the ocean, he had an arm under her knees and was laying her down on the wide bed. Before she could protest, he unhooked her bikini top, slid the bottoms off, and pulled the covers over her.

Feeling her head resting on a soft pillow, she could no longer stay awake.

"Do you want me to stay here with you?" His voice sounded far away.

"Stay here with you." She repeated his words dreamily, in a whisper.

"Do you want me to stay, Titania?" He leaned over and stroked her forehead.

She was too exhausted to remember that she had vowed to return to their business relationship. All she could rely on at that moment was instinct. Closing her eyes she reached for his hand, pressing it to her lips. It smelled faintly of antiseptic and the sea. "Acheson," she whispered.

Her mind was floating, tossing on the violent waves hurling her into the threatening blackness, but as she felt the warmth of his strong body curl protectively around her, she sank into a tranquil sleep, safe from the malevolent island spirits, safe from the hungry sharks.

chapter 16

TITANIA WAS HAVING a strange dream. In it, she and Acheson were walking through the rain forest, wearing ginger-blossom leis, while hundreds of elfin menehunes danced around them, strewing their path with white gardenia petals.

A harsh ringing crept into her dream. It took a moment before she realized it was the telephone by her bed. "Hello?" she mumbled into the receiver without lifting her head from the pillow.

"Titania?" The young voice sounded hopeful, alert, and wide awake. Unmistakably Dana Vasco. "I've been here for an hour, and I thought I'd better see if you were all right. You're usually here before me."

Forcing one eye open, she spied the clock. It was already ten o'clock and light was pouring into the room. There was a trail of sand on the floor near the bed and the pillow next to hers was indented. In the center was a white gardenia. Its fragrance had snuck into her dream.

"I'm all right," she said, smiling to herself. "How are you?" She yawned and stretched. But moving her toes made her remember the coral cuts, the fright of the shark. She sat up in bed. She had never been late to work a day in her life. What time had Acheson left? He certainly had not missed an hour's worth of work. "Dana, order us a pot of coffee from room service and some of those delicious muffins with pineapple preserves. I'll see you in a few minutes."

"I'm sorry I woke you up."

"I'm glad you did, Dana, really."

A damp bath towel already hung on the rack. Acheson must have helped himself to a shower early in the morning, and she had not heard a thing. She was still covered with sand and sea salt; her long hair was matted stiffly to her head. "No wonder he left in such a hurry," she mused to herself, "if I looked this bad."

Dana was sitting attentively at the cash register, going over her lessons on how to work it. So far Titania had discovered that the cash register was the only thing Dana did not excel in, but she was trying very hard to learn.

"Gee, what happened to your feet, Titania?"

"Coral cuts."

"You went swimming after you left us last night?"

"Don't remind me."

"Boy, coral cuts are awful," said Dana sympathetically. "Mama Vasco said Acheson and Kimo used to get 'em all the time as kids. They were pretty wild, but they've sure calmed down."

"Running a business can do that to you," sighed Titania, taking a long sip of the delicious hot coffee. She wondered briefly how she could ever have been as young and bright-eyed as Dana, yet she had been about that age when she came to Naupaka for the first time. Didn't Acheson realize that the fresh young thing he had fallen in love with had disappeared years ago?

"Titania, I'm still really nervous about selling," said Dana. "We're opening in a few days. I hope I do okay."

"You will. The trick is to make a customer feel comfortable. If it's morning, ask if they'd like a cup of coffee.

If it's noon, suggest that they have a sandwich in the dressing room while they try on clothes. Think of Mama Vasco and how she treats people who come into her home. Act as though whoever just walked in the door is just the person you wanted to see."

A hand slipped around Titania's tiny waist, and she wheeled about to see Acheson smiling down at her. "Am I just the person she wanted to see?"

The memory of their afternoon by the caves flushed Titania's cheeks scarlet. "I've got to talk to you, Acheson."

"You're not happy with the shelves?"

"No, they're perfect."

"The lights in the dressing room?"

"No," she said nervously, "they're fine now."

"You're not happy with the way I doctored your toes?"

She was not in a playful mood. "Can I meet you in your office in a couple of hours?"

"In a couple of hours it will be noon. Meet me upstairs in my suite. I'll have lunch sent up for us."

"Acheson . . ." She wanted to tell him not to make it in his suite, but he was out the door before she could protest. What she had to say could be said anywhere, but it would have been easier without his tiki gods glaring at her.

Fortunately Dana took her mind off that problem for the moment. "Titania, what is the difference between the cut of this Elizabeth Stewart bathing suit and this other one?"

Before Titania could explain, Dana had put down the two swim suits and turned toward the door. Remembering her lesson, she greeted someone with "Good morning, how are you today? I'm sorry, we're not open for business yet, but you're more than welcome to browse around."

Titania smiled inwardly. Dana was sure to be a first-class salesgirl with that kind of charm. But when she turned to see who had walked in, she froze. It was Karin Baldwin.

For the sake of Jeremy Evans, Ltd., Titania forced a smile. "How wonderful to see you, Mrs. Baldwin. When did you arrive at Naupaka?" Her own phoniness was nauseating, but it amused her, nonetheless. "Dana, this is a woman you must know. She's one of our favorite customers at our Beverly Hills store."

"Your favorite, Titania darling?" Karin raised her delicately penciled eyebrows in mock amusement. "Your favorite account, perhaps, but hardly *your* favorite customer. And I arrived at this godforsaken island last night to less than a twenty-one-gun salute. *Quelle nuit!*"

"Would you care for some coffee, Mrs. Baldwin?" Dana asked eagerly.

"How thoughtful of you, dear. Titania must be training you well."

"Oh, she is!" Dana was enthusiastic. "Do you take cream or sugar?"

"I like my coffee and my men at full strength." She looked pointedly at Titania. "I called you last night when I arrived. Jeremy sent some sales slips over for you. Where were you?"

Dana rushed back in with the coffee and put it on a table nearby. "We have muffins, too. Would you like one?"

Titania was glad for Dana's interruptions. But how long could they last? The phone rang by the cash register and Titania started toward it, but Dana, in her eagerness, was quick to pick up the receiver. "It's Mama Vasco," Dana said. "You left your purse at the ranch house last night when you stopped by with Kimo. She says she'll have one of the kids run it over if you need it."

"That's not necessary, there's nothing much in it. Why don't you just bring it in with you tomorrow morning."

Karin Baldwin suddenly regarded Titania with a relieved smile. "So you are having a little affair with Kimo Vasco, eh? I've often considered it myself. For a moment I suspected you might have gone after my Acheson even after my warning. But really, Kimo Vasco was a much wiser choice."

Titania realized that whatever explanation Acheson had given Karin for his absence the night before, he had not mentioned her. Was he afraid of Karin's wrath or was there another reason? Titania was on the verge of clearing up Karin's misconceptions, then thought better of it. It would be wiser to speak to Acheson first. "Be sure to let me know if you're considering Kimo," said Titania dryly, "so I can leave *him* alone. I certainly wouldn't want to infringe on your love life."

"No, you certainly wouldn't, dear." She smiled at Titania coldly.

"Just think how easily I stepped aside when you wanted Jeremy."

"That was frivolous of you. He didn't want a divorce, you know. You might have had a very nice arrangement with him." Mrs. Baldwin pulled a dress from one of the racks as she spoke. "I didn't see *this* in Beverly Hills."

"I'm buying differently for this store. You'll be surprised at the things I have here." Titania was smiling. This was the level on which she preferred to deal with Karin Baldwin.

"Lighter fabrics," commented Mrs. Baldwin. She knew as much about clothes as Titania. "This dress is gorgeous."

"Look at this one. The color is stunning on you and you have those shoes I picked out for you at Gucci."

"Which ones?"

"The red sandals with the single strap."

"Oh, yes!" She laughed. "A single strap and the damn things cost $278."

"You got a bargain. They were on sale."

"So I did."

Titania was already pulling things off the rack, handing them to an awed Dana. "Dana, go put these in the first dressing room for Mrs. Baldwin and order a Bloody Mary for her from room service. We're not officially open, but since she just brought us our sales slips, we'll make an exception."

Mrs. Baldwin had a yellow crepe dress, holding it up to her in front of the mirror. "What do you think of this?"

"Not your color," said Titania with authority, taking it out of her hand.

Mrs. Baldwin sighed and shrugged. "When it comes to clothes, my dear, I do trust you. Do you have anything exciting in a bathing suit?"

They went into the dressing room and Titania brought in some of the new ones that had just arrived. Like most women, trying on new clothes made Mrs. Baldwin communicative. "Oh Titania, darling, this is *me*," she gushed over a hot pink one-piece bathing suit that emphasized the fullness of her bust. "He'll see this and go crazy. Can you imagine that Acheson Lane? After all I've done for him, he says he wants to end our *physical* relationship? Have this bathing suit sent to my room. It's gorgeous." She slipped on a blue silk evening dress. "No, I want something a little more daring—something to dazzle the pants off him, the bastard. Actually, he told me he wanted to end it right after you were here, Titania, so naturally I was suspicious. But one transgression I could forgive. Especially now that I know you're wrapped up in Kimo Vasco. You must have heard about the ruckus I caused last night when I arrived. Poor Kimo was quite at a loss."

"Then you and Acheson patched everything up?" asked Titania, playing the cheerful innocent.

"Not quite," she grumbled while slipping on a white backless dress.

Titania tallied up the entire bill on two sales slips. Dana gasped when she saw the $4,367 total. "It was a bad day," mused Titania as Mrs. Baldwin walked out the door. "She usually spends more."

"I think I learned something from watching you," said Dana tentatively.

"What's that?"

"It's important to keep up an incredible pace. I mean, you didn't slack off with her once. There was always something going on or off her. But you told her to take off a lot of the stuff. You even said you wouldn't sell it to her. Why did you do that?"

Titania smiled. "There's no better way to build trust in a customer, Dana. If you don't like something, don't be afraid to say so. They don't want flattery. They want to *know* they look good."

"It's kind of weird, you and her," said Dana with a confused look.

"How's that?"

"It's obvious you despise each other, and yet she is sure you won't trip her up and have her buy something that makes her look awful."

"I try to keep my personal feelings in check during business hours. In fact, that's another good lesson for you, Dana. Keep your business and your personal relationships separate."

Dana considered the point, then pronounced, "It's not such a good rule."

"It's an excellent rule," said Titania with surprise. She was thinking of what she was going to tell Acheson.

"But if it were, then you wouldn't be coming over to our house." Titania had to laugh when she realized Dana was right. "Like any rule, there have to be exceptions."

As she rushed to his private elevator across the lobby, Titania was wishing that she had made other arrangements to meet Acheson. Suddenly she heard her name. "Titania, darling." The affected intonations belonged only to the inimitable Baldwin. Titania braced herself as the woman wisked across the lobby to her side.

"Darling, do you have a seamstress? That green dress you sent over is a half inch too long. It looks atrocious with the shoes. I'll have to have it shortened for tonight."

Titania searched her mind. It was an important detail that she had overlooked. Of course, women would need things altered. These women did not like anything that didn't fit as though it had been tailor-made. She picked up the hotel phone and called Dana at the store. "Dana, do you think you could handle a hem shortening?"

"Sure. I've always made my own clothes. Mama Vasco is the greatest seamstress, and she taught me. Whatever you need done, just give it to me."

"Dana, you are a godsend! How soon can you be over here? Mrs. Baldwin needs to have that green dress shortened a half inch for tonight."

"Wow!" exclaimed Dana. "She wants to go to all that trouble for a measly half inch?"

"Yes." Titania couldn't say any more because Mrs. Baldwin was standing there beside her.

"Oh, I understand." She giggled. "I'll grab some pins and be right over."

"Good girl."

Mrs. Baldwin seemed to have temporarily lost interest in her dress. Titania could see her tightened stance, as though she were coiled and ready to strike.

"Good afternoon, Acheson darling," she said provocatively.

He was leaving his office and heading toward the elevator not far from where they stood.

"Hello, Karin," he said pleasantly, though Titania could tell he was not at ease.

"I want to speak to you, Acheson," continued Mrs. Baldwin. She walked purposefully to the elevator and pressed the button. The door opened and she stepped boldly in. Her manicured finger was on the "hold open" button and she waited for him to step inside with her.

Titania held her breath as Acheson's eyes narrowed.

"I can't speak to you now, Karin, I have some business to take care of with Mrs. Evans."

"What *I* have to say is more important."

"After lunch, we'll meet for a drink on the veranda," he said slowly. There was an edge of irritation in his voice, but he was still smiling and in control.

Titania thought of how many times she had done the same thing with this woman and dozens of others. Just when you were ready to thump them over the head, instead you continued to defer to them. What tyrannical power rich people can wield, thought Titania. It was easy to understand how politicians could be bought.

"I'll see you later, Karin." Acheson was firm, but Karin Baldwin made no move.

Suddenly Titania saw Dana flying toward them, her long black hair flowing behind her. "Ah, here's Dana to alter your dress."

"Can't you come back later?" Karin Baldwin asked Dana with impatience.

"I'm afraid she won't have time later," Titania intervened quickly. "We've got a whole shipment of dresses from Dallas to ticket."

Karin Baldwin was miserably torn between the need for the perfect dress length and her need to disrupt Acheson's lunch. "Let's have dinner then, Acheson darling." She smiled sweetly at him, stepping out of the elevator.

"Fine." He was relieved to have the immediate problem out of the way.

"Cocktails in my room at eight?" she purred.

"I'm going to be tied up at the construction site until late. How about if I meet you in the lobby at eight-thirty?"

Karin Baldwin's eyelids lowered. She was not pleased, but it was better than nothing. She swept regally across the lobby with Dana in tow.

Acheson spoke in a low tone to Titania as they got into the elevator. "She caused quite a scene last night. There was no chance to tell you about it, but I didn't mention your name. She can be a vicious woman and I didn't want it to affect your business before you've even opened. Once you're established we can announce our marriage to the world."

"Acheson," she began with difficulty.

"I love it when you say my name." He combed her with his sea blue eyes. "Especially when we're making love. Are we going to have a hot lunch?"

In a moment they were walking into his penthouse, surrounded by the primitive tiki gods.

He pulled her to him. "I've been thinking all day how good it would feel to hold you in my arms," he said huskily.

For a moment, she let herself be swept away by her own turbulent emotions. Pressed against him, she had to fight against the same fierce desire that had overcome her at the Menehune Caves.

"No, Acheson," she said sharply and pulled away from him. "Why I wanted to talk to you . . . it's about this."

"Yes, it's wonderful . . . why are you frowning?"

"Because it's got to end. Right now. Before we get in any deeper. It won't work."

A puzzled look crossed his face. "Is it because of Karin? I ended it with her months ago. That's what the big fight was about last night. She was insisting on staying here in the penthouse. Kimo knew it was out of the question. I ended it, Titania, because I don't ever want another woman. You're all I've dreamed of—all my life."

"It won't work," she repeated slowly, blocking out everything she was hearing, trying desperately to steady her frantic heartbeat.

She turned away from Acheson and found herself face-to-face with the carved wooden statue of Maui, who glared at her with a menacing expression.

"How can you say it won't work?"

"You just can't mix business and sex."

"Say you don't love me, Titania. That I can accept. But don't throw an idiotic maxim at me."

"Love has nothing to do with it," she said with exasperation.

"It has everything to do with it, Titania. That's the *only* thing that has to concern us!"

"Don't be a fool, Acheson! You talk about love as though it were something tangible like a store or a . . . a hotel. But love is like the menehunes. Everybody talks about them, but nobody's ever really seen them. You look at me and you see a seventeen-year-old girl, full of innocence and mystery, an unattainable fairy princess. *Look* at me, Acheson. I'm a twenty-nine-year-old woman.

I'm made of flesh and disappointments and heartbreaks. At seventeen I would have flown across the waves with you. I saw you as a glorious golden sea god. But you're a mortal, just like I am. Sure, we have a tremendous physical attraction for each other. People have that every day. In a magical kingdom it could last forever, but in everyday life with payrolls to meet, demanding customers to placate, luxury villas to build, our so-called love would crumble into never-never land."

As she spoke, Acheson began to smile. "I don't see what you find so amusing," she said with irritation. "I'm trying to make a serious point and you're not even listening."

He leaned over and brushed her cheek with his lips. "You're more beautiful now than you were at seventeen, Titania. But dumber." His blue eyes were twinkling with mirth. "You claim not to believe in the menehunes and yet when you heard the footsteps coming through the rain forest, you clung to me, shaking with fear."

"It could have been *anybody*." She hedged.

"Titania, before I'm finished with you, you will be believing in menehunes, and love."

"Well, think whatever you want, but I am not going to continue with you."

"We'll see about that." He drew her close and felt her tremble. She pulled away quickly, but the effect had already registered and she flushed deeply as her pulse quickened. He laughed.

"Never." She met his eyes in a defiant challenge.

A waiter arrived with lunch, and as soon as he left, Acheson led her to the table, holding out her chair. "Tell me, Titania. If I had not rushed off last night, would you still feel this way?"

"Of course!" she said with hesitation.

"I doubt it."

"I would have come to my senses. It's an impossible situation."

"It doesn't have to be."

"You're having dinner with Karin Baldwin tonight. It would be a good time to make amends with her," said Titania coldly.

"It *is* Karin Baldwin that has you in a snit, isn't it?" he asked wisely.

"Karin Baldwin is bound to put me in a snit, no matter what she does. But that has nothing to do with the subject, which is you and me," Titania said with exasperation.

"A delightful subject." He smiled engagingly.

"Acheson," she said quietly, "it's *over*."

Her sudden composure threw him off for a moment. "We come back to the heart of the matter, after all, don't we?"

She wasn't sure what he meant.

"The reason you hate Karin Baldwin is that she pried your husband loose. You're not over that jealousy. Am I right?"

Titania looked down at her plate and nodded. "It's not easy to forget or forgive. Perhaps if I thought she really loved him like I did, but it was the mere conquest she wanted . . ."

Acheson stood up from the table and gazed out at the ocean. "I'll never have you until you're free of him," he said almost to himself. "All this talk of sex and business means nothing. You may not know it, but I do. And the damnable thing about it is that I have no way to combat it." He turned back and studied her. "*I* know you don't love him. Trouble is, *you* don't know it yet." He smiled at her. "And I've pushed you too quickly. It was a mistake. Eventually, you'll see that I'm right, my beautiful princess."

She could not answer him. Part of her desperately wanted to believe what he said. Her feelings for him were so strong, but so were her memories of Jeremy. As usual, Acheson had pierced to the core of her problems.

When she got back to the store, Dana had almost finished hemming the dress. Titania looked over her shoulder and saw that she was doing superb work. "How lucky I've been to find you. Did the formidable Baldwin give you any trouble?"

"No, she was too busy complaining about Acheson. She blabbed on and on about him. What a lady. She talks about her old husband and all these other lovers, too, like it was nothing."

"Mrs. Baldwin collects lovers like some women collect butterflies," explained Titania. "Even my husband was in her collection."

"Wow. What a hobby! She's really very beautiful though," conceded Dana. "I can see why men would go for her."

"And her husband's bank is very beautiful, too," added Titania sarcastically.

"Yea, I guess that's why Acheson was fooling around with her, though he never struck me as the kind of guy who would do it for money, you know? I mean, it's sort of a gigolo kind of thing."

Titania bristled at the suggestion. "I'm sure the Baldwin Bank of Beverly Hills went on more than Mr. Baldwin's wife's say-so in advancing him the money for this project."

"Acheson may be in trouble on that," said Dana cautiously.

"In trouble with the bank? Why?"

"Maybe I shouldn't say anything." Dana held back. "I don't know much about financial things. But I think

Acheson's construction costs went way over, and he's asked the bank to loan him more money to complete the hotel. Mrs. Baldwin said something about holding out unless he comes around. Do you suppose that she means she can hold up his bank loan unless he goes back to her?"

"I wouldn't put it past her, though I can't imagine the bank not giving him more money to complete a project they already started. Unless they . . . oh, my lord! They hold the mortgage on the island. Maybe they'll just sit back and wait for him to fail so he'll have to turn over the island! There's no way he can pay back the money he borrowed until the new construction is completed."

"Couldn't he get money from another bank?"

Titania shrugged. "I don't know. I probably know as much about financial things as you do. Jeremy always handled the paperwork on bank dealings. One thing is certain, Karin Baldwin wouldn't threaten to destroy him unless she was sure she could."

Dana looked at her wanly. "Jeez, Titania, that's exactly what she said, that she would destroy him."

chapter 17

TITANIA PICKED UP the phone and dialed Acheson's extension. His secretary told her he was at the construction site and that she would try to reach him if it were urgent. "No, that's okay, I'll go there myself."

She found him on the top floor of the new building, arguing with a contractor about the slipshod way the carpet was being laid. His blue eyes brightened as soon as he saw her. "You've reconsidered already?"

"Acheson," she said breathlessly, brushing her long hair out of her eyes as he walked her out to a balcony. A spectacular vista stretched out before them.

"It's about Karin Baldwin. Dana just told me. She's going to stop your loan."

"Hell hath no fury," he said soberly. "If only the construction costs hadn't run over. I should never have gotten involved, but she had the most attractive interest rates of any woman I'd ever met," he mused.

"Can't you get the money from someplace else? Another bank?"

"I already thought of that. Kimo told me about a Japanese bank in Honolulu that loans money to dogs who need flea collars and accepts dog biscuits as collateral, but they wouldn't even give me a quarter for a cup of coffee. This whole venture is risky. I've got the only hotel on the island. No regular airline services the island. And I'm not willing to open it up to any chain operations or franchise any restaurants. It's difficult, even in Beverly Hills, for a banker to understand the nature of a business like Naupaka. Luckily Karin Baldwin understood it and was able to convince her husband. But now if she withdraws her support..." He pushed his fingers through his thick blond hair, then shrugged. "We'll get married anyway up at Menehune Caves—that is, unless you have anything against marrying a man who's bankrupt."

"But, Acheson, you could solve it all so easily. She's just holding the carrot in front of your nose."

"You mean take her back?" He looked at Titania with surprise.

"Well, yes."

"How quick you are to throw me into the arms of another woman, Titania!" He grinned. "Look, I got along before I had this hotel; I'll get along without it. But not without you. You're all that really matters to me."

"Acheson, don't be a fool! I told you we were finished and I meant it."

"No, you didn't." He smiled confidently in a way that exasperated her. "Or you wouldn't have run over here to warn me about Karin Baldwin."

Titania felt a wave of panic. Didn't he see how desperate his situation was? He stood to lose everything he'd ever worked for. And all because of a woman who was still hopelessly in love with another man. She had to make him see how wrong he was. She thought quickly. "You forget that the failure of Naupaka also means the failure of my store." She managed the cool tone of a businesswoman. "I may not have as much at stake as you do—but it's just as important to me and"—she paused to give it the right emphasis—"my partner."

"Yes, your partner," he said under his breath. "I'll take that into consideration." She could see that she had finally shaken him out of his good-humored apathy. He glanced back into the hotel room. "I'll come down to your bungalow tonight after dinner. We can discuss it then," he said impatiently. "If I don't get back into that room, those idiots are going to carpet the ceiling."

Titania knew she had wounded him and felt miserable about it. The last thing she wanted to do was hurt him, but it was the only way to make him come to his senses and consider his best interests.

By evening the store was ready for the grand opening that was to take place in a few days. There were still some windows to dress, but she was sure it would be ready in time. It was quite a feeling of accomplishment, having managed it all by herself this time.

When she and Jeremy had opened the first store, it had been a joint effort. With a tinge of nostalgia she remembered how they had fallen into bed exhausted every night after having feverishly worked to put the place in order. She recalled with a smile the wonderful exhilaration of being in love and building something together.

As she ate a quiet dinner in her bungalow, she began to think about that first store and her marriage. It was no wonder she could still be in love with Jeremy. Those days had been among the best of her life.

Though her friends told her not to blame herself for the breakup of the marriage, she would always secretly wonder if her own behavior hadn't triggered his affairs. Were there moments she should have been more loving and less concerned about the sales receipts? Should she have been less nakedly ambitious and more nakedly sensual?

Was Karin Baldwin right? Should she have held onto Jeremy, tolerating his infidelities, pretending to look the other way?

And Acheson Lane, who was so utterly naive about love... Thinking about him made her tremble involuntarily. She had such strong feelings for him. He was trying to convince her that what she felt for him was love and what she felt for Jeremy was nothing but rage and anger.

But what did Acheson know about those early days when she and Jeremy were first opening the store? There was no mistaking that for real love. She wondered if a person could ever really recover from such a love.

There was a knock at the door. Could it be Acheson so early? She looked at the clock. It was only nine. He couldn't have finished dinner that fast, especially with all he had to discuss with Karin Baldwin.

The knocking persisted and she rose to answer it.

"Surprise, luv!" Jeremy was standing there with a dozen red roses and a bottle of champagne.

She blinked her eyes to see if the vision would vanish, as though she had brought it on herself by thinking about him. But he continued to stand there smiling at her.

"Well, duckie, aren't you going to invite in an old pal?"

"What brings you so far out of your way, duckie?" she echoed him dryly. The tender nostalgic feelings she'd had earlier seemed to evaporate at the sight of him.

He marched past her, dropping the dozen roses in the kitchen sink, and set to work on opening the Mumm's champagne. "Grand opening's in a few days. I thought you could use some help—at least to celebrate. What a bash we threw to celebrate the first opening. Couldn't let this second venture of ours go by without a nod, could I? Stand out of the way, sweet lady, this is going to pop." He held the bottle away from him and the cork flew across the room toward the door and landed against Acheson Lane's broad chest.

chapter 18

OH, ACHESON, THIS is Jeremy," stammered Titania.

"*The* Acheson Lane, no doubt," said Jeremy, pouring him a glass of champagne. "Charmed to make your acquaintance. Won't you join us in a toast to our new store?"

"Yes," said Titania nervously, "please do, Acheson. How was your dinner?"

"Mrs. Baldwin was not the most pleasant company," he said slowly, loosening his tie.

Titania held her breath. "Mrs. Baldwin didn't . . . ?"

"Mrs. Baldwin!" Jeremy snapped his fingers. "I forgot the dear lady was here. What's her room number? We'll ring her up and have her come down so we can all celebrate. It's not every day we open a new store and it's not every day I venture into the tropics. Good God, woman, it's humid. Don't you have an air conditioner or something?" He picked up the telephone and asked the operator for Mrs. Baldwin's room.

"Jeremy," said Titania sharply. "It's not a good idea to call her."

"Don't be silly, luv. Hello, Karin? Yes. It's Jeremy, I just arrived. . . . What? You sound terribly nasal. How could you be nasal? One never catches colds in Hawaii. State edict against it. What? You're *crying*?" He put his hand over the receiver. "I don't think she'd be much fun at a champagne party," he whispered to Acheson and Titania, who were watching this one-sided conversation helplessly. "Yes, luv, we'll get together for breakfast tomorrow." He hung up the receiver. "Couldn't understand a thing she said with all that blubbering into the receiver. Mr. Lane, you've finished your champagne already. Here, let me fill your glass."

"No, thank you," said Acheson tightly. "Perhaps I should be going."

Titania didn't want him to leave her alone with Jeremy, but she wasn't sure if she should insist that he stay.

"A pleasure to meet you, Jeremy," Acheson said pleasantly in his hotel-owner voice. "I hope you'll enjoy your stay. If there's anything I can do for you, let me know. Are you staying in the main hotel or in one of the bungalows?"

Jeremy shrugged. "I just arrived. Haven't even been to the front desk. I was sure my ex-wife would be her usual hospitable self and invite me to share her bed and bungalow. She's so surprised and delighted to see me. Isn't that right, duckie?"

There was sarcasm in his voice, but one had to know Jeremy well to detect it. Acheson raised his eyebrows and looked at Titania. She flushed crimson.

Jeremy walked over to Titania and put an arm around her shoulders with an easy familiarity. "People always wonder how she and I manage to work so well together after a divorce. But you see here—the picture of compatability."

Titania looked from one man to the other, unable to speak. Acheson's expression told her that he was taking everything Jeremy said for the gospel truth. She desperately wanted to correct the impression, but the thought of Karin Baldwin made her stop. It was Titania's last chance to force Acheson back to the woman who held his future at the end of her purse strings.

"May I speak to you a moment outside?" Acheson turned to Titania.

"Sure." She shrugged. "Be back in a moment, duckie," she called back affectionately to Jeremy.

"So you invited him over here. Why didn't you tell me that yesterday at the caves?" Acheson could not conceal his fury.

"Acheson, I . . . . ah, he came over for the grand opening."

"So you knew all along he'd be here. Hell, it's my own fault, I should have listened to what you've been telling me. You're right, I was believing my own dreams. He's the reason you're so afraid to lose your investment. It's all for Jeremy Evans. The minute he reappears, you fall back into his arms. Without seeing him in the flesh, without seeing you together, I could believe you really loved me." Acheson's neck muscles were taut, his blue eyes sparkling with an inner rage he could barely surpress. "But I want to hear it from your lips, Titania. Tell me right now that you still love him, and I'll never bother you again."

Titania stared up at Acheson's sculptured face, the thick blond hair blowing wildly in the trade winds. She was certain now beyond any doubt that she loved him with a passion she never had, even in the best days, for Jeremy Evans. The man inside her bungalow was a stranger, a bad dream she had already forgotten. Everything she ever wanted was Acheson Lane. He was the love she had been destined for all her life.

But to tell him that would be to condemn him to lose Naupaka. It would be like losing half his life. Though she longed to throw her arms around his neck and tell him the truth, the image of Karin Baldwin held her back.

She had to convince Acheson she was still in love with her ex-husband. It was the only way to make him patch things up with Karin. For all his talk about putting his love for her first, Titania knew that was the stuff of fairy tales. It might carry him for a few months or years. But with every minor disagreement, he would begin to look on her as the woman for whom he had sacrificed everything. Eventually the smoldering resentment would burst into flames and consume their love.

She would not be the Lady of Darkness who destroyed the great god Maui. She loved him far too much to make him unhappy.

Though it pained her, she said, "Yes, Acheson. I still love him." Without looking at him again, she walked back into the bungalow.

"So that's the heartbreaker, eh?" Jeremy changed his tone to cynicism as soon as Acheson was well out of sight.

"Heartbreaker?"

"Yes." He stretched out on her couch and put his feet up on the coffee table, surveying the room. "Karin Baldwin called me last night and I decided to hop a plane over to have a look-see."

"Why you two-faced, slippery..." Titania flushed with anger. "'Just thought I'd stop in to help you celebrate.'" She imitated his British accent. "Why aren't you up in dear Karin's room consoling her then?"

"Because she was having dinner with Mr. Lane when I arrived, luv. I thought she'd managed to straighten things out. But evidently she hadn't. Curious how he popped in over here after having dinner with her. Or is it so very curious, my duckie dear?"

He gave her a sly, sidelong glance. "That hotel owner looked rather taken with you. Been sneaking furtive kisses beneath the palm trees these torrid tropical nights?"

"You're disgusting, Jeremy," she said in a barely audible voice.

"Ah! So I'm right! The Baldwin suspected as much when you were both missing last night. The plot thickens." He twisted an imaginary mustache melodramatically. "Just what I always said you needed. You see, it wasn't so hard to get your dainty webbed feet wet, was it, duckie?"

She regarded Jeremy with undisguised loathing, wondering how she could ever have thought she loved him. "Jeremy, you think of sex as something you acquire like a new suit. Did it ever occur to you that people's feelings are involved?"

"Feelings are so unfashionable this season, rather like wide lapels." He shrugged. "Why can't you simply accept it like any other physical activity, like skiing or tennis or jogging. It's a natural bodily function that's been around a lot longer than any of those other sports."

She shook her head. "You'll never change."

"Well, at least *I* have never made love to anyone for money."

"And what is *that* supposed to mean?"

"Don't shout, my dear. You'll wake up all those exotic birds that are supposed to be fluttering around here in paradise. A paradise, I might add, that has been bought and paid for by a *very* teary-eyed Baldwin. Not getting much return on her investment, I'd say. Bring me the bottle of champagne, will you, luv?"

She wanted to send it crashing down on his head. How dare Jeremy put Acheson in that category? "And I don't suppose *you* gave her account with *us* a thought when you were escorting her to dinner at the Rangoon

Racquet Club, writing the check off on our income taxes as an entertainment expense?"

"You defending him?" Jeremy raised his dark eyebrows and looked at her with amusement.

"What if I am?"

"Well?"

"It's none of your business."

"There, you are wrong. We are still business partners, Titania," he said soberly, putting his feet back on the floor. "Your *personal* life is no concern to me at all. But this little affair you're having with Mr. Lane is threatening our business investment. If the Baldwin Bank pulls out, he's up the proverbial creek without a paddle, and we both know that if he drowns, he takes our store with him."

Titania sat down in the chair opposite Jeremy. They were now on a level she could deal with. When he was playing the sassy ex-husband, he was impossible. The sober, levelheaded businessman, concerned about their investment, was an entity she could come to terms with. "I'll be honest with you, Jeremy. I did get carried away with Acheson Lane. But I realized how foolish it was and I told Acheson it was all a mistake. I've had enough of being involved with a man I also have to face in a business relationship."

Jeremy was sipping his champagne calmly, but his mind was working. "Does she know definitely that you're the one he was with yesterday?"

"No. She thinks I'm seeing the general manager, Kimo."

"Well, that's good news. She's a vindictive woman and if she thought *you* were stealing Acheson away, she might start buying her dresses elsewhere."

"Is that all that concerns you?" she shot angrily at

him. "That we might *lose* a few dollars."

"About three thousand dollars every month," Jeremy corrected her.

"I love this double standard," sighed Titania with exasperation. "She can seduce my husband before my very eyes; but let *me* have an innocent affair with one of her lovers and all of a sudden she's Pele, the volcano goddess, spewing fire and lava."

"What quaint little localisms you've picked up." Jeremy smiled. "Well, when you're as rich as Mrs. Baldwin, you can afford to live by a double standard."

"A purely selfish standard," muttered Titania.

"The newly rich are noted for being rather ungenerous with their possessions," he mused. "Now, Titania, calm down. We've got to consider this thing rationally. None of this is making much sense. I must have missed some essential detail. Why in the world did Lane break off with as 'lucrative' a mistress as Karin Baldwin?"

"Because he's in love with me. He wants to marry me."

Jeremy looked at her oddly. "Fine if he loves you and wants to marry you, but why should that preclude his continuing with Madame Baldwin?"

Titania sighed. "I wouldn't expect you to understand something like that."

"It's so nineteenth century!" He shrugged. "Well, be that as it may, as long as you've told him you're through, that should reopen the door to *chez* Baldwin. He's probably back with her right now, let's hope. I don't know about you, but this whole thing for me has been most fatiguing." He started to unbutton his shirt.

"Jeremy, you're *not* spending the night here."

"I have to sleep somewhere." He yawned.

"There's a nice big sandy beach just down that path." She was pointing to it.

"Your hospitality is overwhelming. Let me check on the blubbering Baldwin. If he's going to spend the night with her, he should be there by now." He dialed the extension directly this time, without going through the operator. No doubt, thought Titania, he knew it all along. "Hello, Karin, me' love. You don't sound nearly so nasal. Don Juan there? No? Well, to hell with him. Put on something pretty and sexy and I'll see you in a few minutes."

"That didn't take you long," said Titania dryly.

"Believe me, I'd rather stay here. But I can't wait all night for an invitation, can I?" He buttoned up his shirt.

"You could wait for the next century and still not get an invitation."

"Rather what I thought." He plucked one of the long-stemmed red roses from the sink. "You won't miss one, will you?"

Before she could tell him what to do with all of them, he was almost out the door. "Your handsome hotel owner is a fool, Titania. I should have listened to you in the first place. We should never have gotten ourselves involved here."

She threw the empty champagne bottle in the garbage next to the dozen roses, minus one, and lay back on her bed. Only last night, she remembered, Acheson had lain next to her, protecting her from sharks and demons and ex-husbands. It would be easy to pick up the phone and dial his extension now. A longing for him welled up inside her. To run her hands through his thick hair, to hear his low voice whisper her name, to feel the hardness of his strong chest as he lay against her. She reached for the phone, hesitated, then dialed. There was no answer. Had he gone back to Karin Baldwin after all? Would he meet Jeremy there?

chapter 19

WHATEVER HAD GONE on in the Baldwin suite, Titania did not learn until morning when Jeremy wandered into their store. "Nice job." He glanced around with approval. "Very nice, indeed. Got any coffee?"

Dana hurried to get him a cup. "She's a pretty young thing," he told Titania. "Where'd you find her?"

"She's Kimo's niece. And she's only seventeen."

"Glad you told me. Her being seventeen wouldn't bother me, but having to tangle with Kimo would. Rather muscular fellow. She'd make a great model."

"I know. I'm going to have her model during lunch on the veranda, take around Jeremy Evans, Ltd. cards. I also thought I'd have her wear our clothes in the store, change off every few hours. Anything she wears I'm sure would sell in a minute."

"Well, before you make any more plans," he sighed, "we'd better talk." He sat down in one of the rattan chairs and sipped his coffee. "Your gallant hotel owner, of course, never showed up at Baldwin's room last night. He didn't wander back down to your bungalow, did he?"

"No."

"Well, he could still salvage this place if he wanted to make up to her. She's ready to be gracious and forgive him all his sins. In a way, she's a rather pitiful character, for all her beauty and money."

"About as pitiful as Lady Macbeth," Titania sniped. "Don't shed any tears. I'm sure she'll find another 'investment' before long."

Jeremy smiled brightly at her. "She has."

Titania looked at him with horror. "You?"

"Jeremy Evans, Ltd." He began to talk excitedly. "You know how we always wanted to buy the linen shop next door and expand? Well, she's going to get us an incredible loan at an interest rate that's so low it's obscene!"

"That brazen woman dangles her 'obscene' interest rates in front of men like some women dangle..."

"Titania, this is the opportunity of a lifetime! Leave this crazy Hawaiian venture before we lose our shirts and come back to Beverly Hills. Before long we'll be an outfit like Giorgio." Jeremy's dark eyes were brilliant. "Besides, you'll melt away over here in this blasted humidity, miles away from civilization."

"I rather like it here," she protested.

"If it's that hotel owner you're thinking about, forget it. He's not for you."

"Who are you to judge what's for me?"

"I know you. I lived with you, remember? That guy may have been bright enough to build this whole thing, but he's not bright enough to carry it through or he would have patched things up with Baldwin. You need a man like...like..." He paused to take a sip of coffee.

"*You?*" She laughed cynically. "We've been through this one before."

"I still love you, Titania. Why won't you believe that?"

"Because if you loved me, you wouldn't have wanted Karin Baldwin and ten other women."

"I'd give them all up to have you back." He stood up and put his arms around her, gazing with sadness into her eyes. "I've been miserable since you've been over here. The Beverly Hills store just isn't the same. The life, the fun's gone out of it."

With amazement Titania realized she felt nothing. The pulsing, trembling heat she'd always felt in Jeremy's arms was gone! There was a time she would have crawled on her hands and knees to hear him say this. Now it meant nothing.

Jeremy continued, unaware of her indifference. "I know you still love me, Titania. I knew it all along and I took you for granted. You wanted to come over here to test me—see if I'd come around. Well, it worked. I've missed you so much I could cry. Then I saw you with that guy—that idiot—and I knew I had to have you back."

"You were jealous?" Titania's mouth fell open.

"You have no idea." He moved forward to kiss her but she pulled back.

"Tell me, Jer," she said softly, gazing into his dark eyes, "would you give up Mrs. Baldwin and her dangling interest rates to have me back?"

He took a moment before answering. "Well luv, there's no reason we couldn't wait until her loan went through..."

She walked away from him and smiled wearily. "That's what I thought."

"But that doesn't mean I don't love you."

"I suppose perhaps you do—in your own twisted way, Jeremy, but it's not enough."

Jeremy took a deep breath and bit his lower lip. "All right then, luv. To the devil with the Baldwin and her dangling interest rates! Just come back to Beverly Hills—come back to me."

Titania shook her head. "You're about a month too late."

"Come on, you're not in love with this . . . this hotel owner, are you? He may be good for a romantic fling, but . . ."

"Whether or not I'm in love with him is beside the point. I am not in love with *you* anymore." She had never seen Jeremy look so downcast. For the first time in his life, he'd been trapped by his own game. Since he'd treated her badly for so long and she'd taken it, he could not understand what had gone wrong.

"Well," he muttered under his breath. "I'll . . . uh, go on up to the hotel bar, maybe and . . ."

"Nothing doing," she said briskly. "You came over here to help me open the store. We're still partners, you know, and we're opening tomorrow. Help me get these dresses sorted and marked."

He seemed relieved. She may not love him, but she was not casting him out. "We're friends then, eh, luv?"

"Of course we're friends. And we're partners." She held her hand out to him and he took it between both of his.

"Friends." He kissed her lightly on the cheek and went into the back room. "This is a disaster, luv!" he called out cheerfully. "Good thing I'm here."

Titania put some dresses out on the rack and smiled to herself. If no other good came of this venture, at least it had cured her of that impossible, destructive love for Jeremy.

He was still busy in the back room organizing stock when Karin Baldwin strode in, looking calm and fresh despite the tears of the night before. Jeremy might be able to pity this woman, but Titania never would.

"Good afternoon, Titania, I've come to fetch Jeremy for lunch." She smiled at her with cold detachment.

"He's in the back. I'll get him."

She found Jeremy rearranging the boxes of sandals. "It'll be easier if the lower sizes are on the lower shelves where you can reach them," he said without turning around.

"There's a lady outside who's come to *fetch* you, Jer." She emphasized the word, then added comically, "Is she also going to teach you how to sit up and heel?"

Jeremy smiled wryly at the image. "I rather think 'roll over' for my kibble is more like it. This place is fairly well in order. I don't see where you'll need any more help this afternoon. Think I'll relax and enjoy the scenery."

Titania regarded him with surprise. "*You* are going to venture out of an air-conditioned room?"

"I didn't say that, luv. There's a lovely view from the lady's window."

With a secret joy, Titania realized that for the first time she was able to joke around with her ex-husband, even about Karin Baldwin, and not experience the fearful heart tremors of the past. Jeremy seemed to notice it, too. "Tani," he said warmly. It was a nickname of endearment he had not used in a long time. "I think we've reached another plateau. Let's hold onto it."

She nodded with a smile of understanding. "I guess it's time."

He gave her the "V for victory" sign and went out to join Mrs. Baldwin.

Titania took a deep breath and let it out. How simple it all was, she mused, once you understood your own feelings. Acheson had been right about it all along.

Acheson. How her insides ached with longing for him. But she knew she'd been right to send him away. It was the only way he'd see the importance of keeping his hotel. Deep down, men were practical, she told herself.

Even Jeremy had acted briefly as though his life were coming to an end when she said she didn't love him, and hadn't he bounced back quickly? This very moment he was enjoying himself with another woman. Acheson could do the same thing. He *must*.

It was dark by the time she and Dana closed up, but the store was in perfect order, ready for the grand opening tomorrow afternoon. Was it futile to open when the hotel might not last? They had signed a year's lease. If worse came to worst, they could always close the store and pay it off. There would be a loss but not a catastrophe. Only Acheson stood to lose everything.

Kimo joined her on the garden path as she headed toward her bungalow. She was glad to see him. "I haven't seen Acheson around today," she began uneasily, hoping he'd fill her in.

"You wanted to see him?" Kimo glanced at her hopefully.

"I was worried about his loans."

"That's all, eh?"

"What do you mean?"

Kimo wore a pained expression. "You have no idea what you did to him. He loves you, Titania. He'd give up the world to have you."

"But I couldn't let him do that," she said helplessly. "Kimo, I love him too much for that. If he continued on with me, he'd never go back to Mrs. Baldwin and he'd lose everything he's worked for all these years. That's why I told him I was still in love with Jeremy."

Kimo threw back his head and laughed. "You only told him what you did—to get him to go back to Karin Baldwin?"

She was unable to meet his gaze. "Please don't tell him, Kimo. He might still do it."

"But you really do love him?" Kimo pressed her.

She sighed. "I can't tell you how much. But if we got married, eventually he'd despise me for making him give up his island. I'm sure even the Duke of Windsor had some regrets."

"Acheson's not the Duke of Windsor," laughed Kimo, "and he's in no danger of losing anything!"

"But the new loan from the Baldwin Bank?"

Kimo shook his head. "After he talked to you he placed a call to Beverly Hills and spoke directly to Mr. Baldwin. The loan had already been approved that morning. Mrs. Baldwin would have been too late even if she'd wanted to cause some mischief. The Baldwin Bank has too much invested here already to let it falter."

Tears of joy sprang to Titania's eyes and she hugged Kimo impulsively. "But where's Acheson? I've got to talk to him."

"You're going to have to wait. He's gone off to Palikaho Beach."

"Where is it? Couldn't we go there now?"

"No way to get there by jeep. No roads in."

"Then what about by boat?"

"Not at night. It's too dangerous. Acheson took off last night like a lunatic. I've never seen him in such a crazy mood. He got into an outrigger, threw in some food and beer, and paddled off. He might be crazy enough to try and get there at night, but I don't think even Kui, skilled as he is, would take you. There are too many shallow rocks. A boat could get dinged up pretty bad."

"But I've got to talk to him. I don't want him to keep thinking I don't love him."

Kimo slipped a friendly arm around her shoulders. "Hey, why don't you come back to the ranch tonight for dinner? Tomorrow morning I'll have Kui take you to Palikaho."

Sensing it was futile to insist, she agreed. Being with Mama and Papa Vasco would help keep her mind occupied.

Kui was also there for dinner, and after most of the kids were sent to bed, the adults sat out on the veranda, sipping rum drinks and swapping stories about the hotel and plantation. Titania found it hard to concentrate, for her mind was floating around the island to Palikaho Beach.

"Is Palikaho very far?" she asked Kui on the short ride back to the hotel.

"It's around the south side of the island." He took another swig of beer. "Not easy to get to, but body surfing there is incredible. You like to body surf?"

"No, I was justing thinking..."

"I know what you're thinking," laughed Kui. "I was just teasing you. I'll take you there first thing in the morning."

"You wouldn't think of taking me tonight, would you?" she asked hopefully.

"At night? Crazy *wahine*! Look, I saw Acheson take off there last night, but he is crazy enough to do something like that. Always was, eh Kimo? Remember the time he talked us into taking those girls hiking up the Awaawapuhi Trail in Kauai?"

Kimo laughed. "It got so hot, we decided to take all our clothes off and there we were, all stark naked and the park rangers coming after us. Those were the days—to be young and crazy again, eh, man?"

"Hey, we're not so old. Maybe you are, but I've got a few good years of hell-raising left."

"From the way you talked earlier," said Titania slyly,

"I thought you were ready to collect your old-age pension."

Kui looked at her and grinned. "No wonder Acheson likes you. You're just like he is, get a harebrained idea in your head and you don't let go. What do you say, Kimo? Let's take her to Palikaho."

"Kui! This time of night?"

"We've gone out later than this, man. There's a full moon at least."

"You're out of your mind." Kimo pulled the jeep into the parking lot.

"Kimo, you're gettin' old," taunted Kui. "Never would have thought that."

"Come on, Kui," Kimo said, with a little irritation. "For you and me to risk our necks is one thing, but not with Titania."

"We'll take an outrigger. It's safer than an outboard. Even Acheson took a canoe last night." Titania's heart raced. She could see Kimo's will weakening.

"Crazy wahine." He laughed and took her hand. "Come on, before we change our minds."

In a minute the three of them were running down the beach toward the outriggers.

chapter 20

KUI SHOWED HER how to hold the paddle. "It's fourteen on the right, fourteen on the left—just like the song. Kimo's the hot shot—on a paddling team in Honolulu."

The bottom of her short muu-muu got wet as she waded into the water, and she tried to hold it up. "It's gonna be soaked through by the time we get there." Kimo laughed. "You still want to go?"

She let the hem drop into the water and climbed into the hull, taking the center place in the small canoe. "Are you sure an outboard wouldn't be better?" she ventured.

"The original Hawaiians crossed the entire Pacific in these," scoffed Kui.

She decided to be quiet or they might change their minds. But once they were bounding over the waves, she knew that what she had talked them into doing was insane. Despite their early reluctance, Kui and Kimo were having a wonderful time.

"Jus' like the ol' days, eh Kimo?—when we used to go out with the boss, surf till morning. What he want to go and build this big resort for?"

Part of what was adding to their good time were the bottles of Primo beer Kimo had lifted from the bar at the beach. Being in the center of the canoe, Titania's job became bartender as she opened the bottles and handed them up front to Kui and back to Kimo. On their third beer, the two of them began to sing, teaching her choruses in Hawaiian she knew were off-color by the way they howled with laughter.

"Used to be thousands of canoes in old Hawaii," Kui told her. "They say three thousand went out to greet Captain Cook's ships when they came into Kealakekua Bay. Canoe-making was a religious ritual. You make one mistake on *mana* or 'good luck' of the canoe and the maker was in danger."

"Did you guys used to go to Palikaho often?" Titania asked.

"Yes. Good waves, nice beach, mango and banana trees. Come to think of it, what else do you need in life, hey Kimo?"

"We're almost there," he yelled back. "Now's when we gotta be careful for the rocks. There's one spot we can catch a wave and go all the way in. Whew, ol' Acheson's gonna be surprised! Paddle hard, wahine, till we got the wave."

She strained her eyes to catch a possible glimpse of Acheson on the beach, but it was too dark to see anything except for some slender palm trees blowing in the wind. Her heart was pounding as they waited silently. Kimo and Kui's eyes were on the ocean, waiting for the set of waves. Suddenly, Kui gave a whoop and they began to paddle. Water splashed her from both sides of the canoe and she dug in with her paddle, trying to keep pace with Kui in front. When they caught it, the salt water drenched her from head to toe, but the wind in her face and the powerful wave curling behind took her breath away.

When they were almost to the shore, the three of them jumped into the water and brought the canoe up onto the sand. Acheson's canoe was close by, but he was not around. Kimo made the cooing birdcall she remembered from the Menehune Caves. It wasn't answered, and he made it again.

Titania felt a wave of fear wash over her. "Where do you suppose he is?" She grabbed Kimo's arm.

"Back in there, somewhere." He pointed into the dense foliage. "Don't look at me that way. I may have brought you here, but we're not tromping through the bamboo to find him."

"But . . ."

"There aren't any paths. We could wander around all night and not find the way out. Sit down. We'll have another beer and think what to do."

Titania suddenly felt tired. It had been a crazy idea—though probably fun for Kimo and Kui. But she ached to see Acheson and her sides were bursting to tell him how much she loved and wanted him.

"There he is," said Kimo, pointing down the beach. He was coming slowly toward them, though she could only see his large frame outlined against the hills; the moonlight made his blond hair glow a supernatural white. He was naked and the way the wind was tossing his hair made him look like a powerful oceanic god who could harness the sun or pull islands up and out of the sea.

Still soaking from the canoe ride, the thin muu-muu clung to her body as she ran. Her damp hair flowed out behind her in the warm night wind. Acheson stared at her, unbelieving, as if she too were an apparition. Then she saw his wide grin as he held his arms out to envelop her.

Kimo and Kui were back in the canoe and paddling out. "Acheson, they brought me here because I wanted to tell you that . . ."

"No, don't talk, now. I just want to feel you near me. Get this wet thing off." They fell together in the sand and he lifted the muu-muu over her head, covering her body with kisses. "You taste of the sea," he whispered, "my beautiful Titania." He brushed the sand from her hips and thighs, caressing them with tenderness, while his lips sought the silky tips of her breasts.

She ran her hands through his thick golden mane, pulling it tight and releasing it as would a cat in ecstasy. She gripped his powerful shoulders, then smoothed her fingers across the taut muscles of his chest covered with the coarse-curled golden hair.

He rolled onto his back and pulled her onto him. She dug her knees into the sand and he held her waist as they imitated the driving rhythms of the violent surf that pounded the nearby rocks. Together they rode the crests of towering waves, plunging into the blue depths, rising up again out of the foam. He was her golden god of the sea and she was his mistress with flowing ribbons of seaweed in her hair that wrapped around them. They danced with fragrant flower leis of moonlight and jeweled garlands of ocean spray.

Dawn came slowly with feathery wisps of lavender clouds stealing over the jagged green cliffs. The miracle of the sunrise hardly seemed less miraculous than their love as they stretched out together on the white sand.

As soon as it was light enough to see, he took her into the dense jungle behind them to pick their breakfast of wild mangoes. They found a lagoon fed by a trickling stream.

He hadn't eaten much of the food he had brought with him from the hotel two nights before. "In a place like this you don't get very hungry."

"What have you been doing all this time?"

"Surfing, thinking." He lay back against a gnarled kukui tree. "What did you do yesterday?"

"Got the store ready to open."

"Jeremy help you?" His face muscles grew taut.

"For a while, but he went up to Karin's room for lunch and that was the last I saw of him. He spent the night before with her, too, after you left."

"I thought he spent it with you." Acheson regarded her strangely.

"I wanted you to think that."

"But why?"

"I figured that if you thought I was still in love with Jeremy, you'd make up with Karin and save your hotel, save the island. I didn't want you to hold it against me for the rest of our lives."

"None of this would mean anything if I couldn't have you, Titania."

"But Naupaka is more than just the resort. You love the Menehune Caves and this beach..."

He waved off the thought. "There are islands all over the world as beautiful, public parks here in Hawaii where hardly anyone ever goes. I could even get my old job back in Bali. You'd love it there. You could always have a store. We'd get by. To create a resort like Naupaka was a dream—but with dreams, one is always in danger of being rudely awakened. You forget I had two dreams, and you'll always be the far more important of the two. Let Karin go sit on her gorgeous assets. I've got the loan anyway."

"I know. Kimo told me. That's why I made him and Kui bring me here. She's told Jeremy she now wants to invest in our store in Beverly Hills so we can expand it."

"Take my advice and get your loan elsewhere. There are far too many strings and clauses attached to her contracts. I should have listened to Kimo—to my lawyers. But the savings in interest alone meant being able to add three more villas. And at that time she had me believing she was an angel. I'll have to admit she did a creditable job with the decor—and getting the right stores in." He smiled at her. "I was just afraid if she found out about you and me, with her vindictive spirit, it might mean the end of Jeremy Evans, Ltd. at Naupaka."

"What does she have to do with Jeremy Evans, Ltd.?" asked Titania with surprise.

"With the loan contracts from the bank, I had to make some concessions to her which her husband insisted on. You see, he may not mind what she does with her time, but when it comes to his bank's money, he's very astute. He knows that she has exquisite taste in clothes, in furnishings. The only way he would invest millions of dollars in an exclusive resort was to make sure it was as elegant as I claimed it would be. That's why the contract specified she was to choose the decorator and oversee the plans for the arcade and new additions. She made sure the villas were every bit as luxurious as those on Bali and other resort hotels of that caliber. She was also to give final approval to Jeremy Evans, Ltd."

"*Was* to? You mean she didn't?"

"Not formally, in writing, as was required by the contract. Kimo reminded me of that clause after you'd signed the lease. After she saw us at the airstrip that day, she raised hell about you. She was sure that's why I ended my affair with her. She threatened not to sign the approval then reconsidered when she discovered she'd left some dress behind and there was no place here she could buy one. Even then, she never actually signed the paper."

"Why didn't you tell me any of this?" Titania was thinking now as a businesswoman and was angry at his deception. "It wasn't fair of you to let us sign a lease that might not be legally binding. After all, we've invested a lot of money in that store."

He pulled her to him. "I would have done anything

to get you back here. I can always reimburse you or pay lawyers' fees, but I can't find another princess. Hey, what are we doing lazing around here?" He held her away from him and planted a kiss on the end of her nose. "Your store is opening at five this afternoon. I've got cases of champagne on ice for this occasion."

She could not stay angry. Standing on her tiptoes, she reached up and kissed him. "To hell with the store," she sighed. "Let's just stay here. Baldwin will probably have a detachment of lawyers waiting for us as we paddle up to the beach." She didn't know how close she was to the truth.

"Then we'll use the occasion to announce our engagement. It's a sin to let champagne go to waste."

chapter 21

SHE DID NOT put her muu-muu back on until they were within sight of the hotel. She would have a terrible sunburn, she knew, but it would only remind her of the enchantment of Palikaho. It was a place, like the Menehune Caves, that she would never forget as long as she lived.

Several hotel guests were on the beach when they arrived, looking like two untamed sea urchins with their hair tangled and clothes drenched from the sea. For those guests who had never seen the owner of Naupaka in anything but a white linen suit, this wild, tan, muscled body was quite a shock, as was Titania Evans whom they had only seen looking as though she had stepped out of the pages of *Town and Country*.

But Titania and Acheson were too much in love to care what anybody thought of their appearance. Holding hands like a couple of teenagers, they walked up the beach greeting people happily, telling them to be sure to come to the opening of the new store in the shopping arcade.

As they walked up on the veranda, they saw Jeremy and Karin Baldwin. "Good afternoon," they said cheerfully.

Mrs. Baldwin glared daggers at Titania. "You don't miss a trick, do you, Mrs. Evans. First Kimo, and now his best friend."

"I've never known *you* to keep a scorecard," said Titania offhandedly. She was tired of the hypocracy that kept her maintaining a quiet civility toward this woman, simply because of the size of her charge account.

Jeremy now was glaring at Titania too, but with mortification. For a moment she thought he might be caught in the throes of jealousy. Only yesterday he had confessed his love for her. But then she realized the source of his agitation. It was no longer a secret that she and Acheson were lovers. Karin Baldwin, in her vindictive style, would no longer be willing to invest in Jeremy Evans, Ltd. in Beverly Hills as long as Titania owned half interest.

Acheson kissed Titania lovingly on the cheek. "I've got some things to take care of, princess. See you at the grand opening later."

Mrs. Baldwin's mouth fell open and she stormed off, leaving Jeremy to face Titania.

He accompanied her back to the bungalow. "How could you do this to me?" he whined. "I had everything all set up so beautifully. Couldn't you have waited until after she left? All right, so she doesn't give us a loan to expand. But now she'll never set foot in the Beverly Hills store again! And all those wealthy matrons who follow her advice on everything. Once she starts lying and telling them that our stock has gone down in quality . . . we're finished!"

"Oh, Jeremy, get lost," she moaned. "I'm sunburned and tired and we've got a new store to open in a few hours."

"Now I know you've gone off your blooming rocker! Why not just plead temporary insanity and get it over with. Take a gun and shoot me between the eyes! What have I ever done to you to deserve this?"

She wheeled on him. "You've done plenty, but don't go accusing me of purposely falling in love with Acheson Lane so that I could settle a debt with you."

"Then what else did you go and do such a stupid thing for?"

She suddenly looked at him with pity. "No, I don't suppose I could expect you to accept the existence of that kind of love any more than you'd understand about menehunes."

"Menie-*whoo*nies? Now I know you've gone berserk. The other night it was Pele, the volcano goddess. Did you ever consider that you may be struck with some rare kind of island fever?"

She laughed. "Yes. But isn't it odd that you think *I'm* crazy, and Mrs. Baldwin, who's ranting and raving, you think is sane."

"Karin Baldwin can well afford her eccentricities. You and I aren't rich enough. Titania, you don't know the half of it. She found out last night that you'd gone to see Acheson on that remote beach."

"How did she find out last night?" asked Titania with surprise.

"His friend Kimo couldn't be bought, but Kui sold her the information for a mere twenty dollars. She demanded that he take her there, too. But he said he was too tired. He did offer her one of the canoes and pointed out the direction."

Titania laughed.

"Go ahead and giggle, but she was on the phone to Honolulu. She's having a lawyer fly over here—he'll be arriving any minute. She's determined to stop our store from opening, and she's got some sort of legal document to prevent it. It seems she's to have final approval on every store that goes into the shopping arcade."

"Jeremy, why does this have you upset? You're the one who suggested yesterday we shouldn't open at all."

He shrugged sarcastically. "You're right. Who cares anymore? We're going down the tubes, thanks to you, no matter what happens now."

"Thanks to *me*?" She bristled again. "You could have all the affairs you wanted, and now that we're divorced, and I have one, you're acting like it's the cataclysm of the century!"

"Duckie," he said dryly. "I may have had affairs, but I never put our business in jeopardy over them."

"We all have our little priorities," she sighed. "Now go run off and do something useful. I'll see you at the store at five."

"I'll be at the bar," he muttered and sulked off, suffering more, she suspected, from the humid heat than from his own imagined financial ruin.

Titania ran into the bungalow, picked up the phone, and dialed Acheson's private extension. "Hi. Have you heard? She's got a lawyer coming over."

"He's sitting right here filling me in."

"Shall we go ahead with the store opening?"

"Of course, we'll go ahead. The champagne's on ice. Do you still love me, Titania?"

"More than ever."

"Good. Then see you at the store at five o'clock."

There was a bald man in a dark suit standing in front of the store. It was the attorney, she surmised, though he looked more like a mortician.

"Mrs. Evans," he said in a thin voice, "I suggest you not go in there." He waved a piece of paper in her face. "I have an injunction . . ."

Titania looked at him with concern. "An injunction?

Why, that's terrible. I've heard prunes sometimes are helpful."

"You have no right to open this store," he said tonelessly.

"Well, if you say so." She shrugged. "But I'll bet you a bottle of champagne it doesn't say anything on that piece of paper about us having a party in there."

He slipped on a pair of horn-rimmed glasses and scanned the document. "As long as you don't engage in any business," he pronounced somberly, as though it were an inalterable curse.

"But I've already engaged in business," she said innocently. "I sold about four thousand dollars' of clothes here the other day to a Mrs. Baldwin—the name ring a bell? I see it does. It was a charge-account sale. I've got the receipt inside if you'd like to see it."

The man backed off as though she had brandished a silver cross at him and he headed back toward the hotel tucking the papers into a manila folder as he went, nearly bumping into Acheson Lane coming down the arcade.

"What did you say to him?" laughed Acheson. "The poor little man certainly looks perplexed."

"I told him Mrs. Baldwin bought about four thousand dollars' worth of clothes from me the other day. I offered to show him the receipt."

Acheson hugged her. "If I'm correct, he's headed back to her suite to tell her just how far she can go with that clause." He laughed. "Any court would take a four thousand-dollar purchase as approval."

"Well, be sure to get that lawyer's address," said Titania. "I want him to come to our next Halloween party."

The hors d'oeuvres and champagne began to arrive and were set up exquisitely on long tables throughout the store. It wasn't long after, that the entire Vasco family flocked in—children, grandchildren, and cousins.

The band arrived, and hotel guests began flowing through the door, marveling at the clothes, already picking out things they would like to try on the next day. Jeremy arrived and sat sullenly in a corner, unable to enjoy the festivities. "No sense in celebrating when we'll never be able to open this place without getting slapped with a lawsuit."

"Well, then instead of a grand opening, we shall call this our grand closing," said Titania, giddy with champagne and the feel of Acheson's arm around her. "Don't be so glum, Jeremy, the lawyer was here. I don't think Karin has a case, and even if she does, we'll sell all these clothes in Beverly Hills if we don't sell them here. If the lease is void, we don't have to pay anything on it. We'll have lost some money but nothing tragic."

Suddenly the room grew silent as faces turned toward the door. Mrs. Baldwin was coming toward them, her head held aristocratically high. She was dressed in a shimmering white dress. Her lawyer, expressionless, stood slightly behind her, manila folders in his hand. Mrs. Baldwin made her way through the crowd toward Acheson and Titania. Ignoring Acheson, she faced Titania. "May we have a few words?"

"Sure," said Titania.

"Jeremy," Mrs. Baldwin called over her shoulder, "I'd like to speak to you, too."

The three of them went back into one of the fitting rooms, where they surprised Dana and a young lifeguard in an embarrassed embrace. "Take my advice and watch out for lifeguards, Dana." Titania laughed as she and the boy flitted by them.

After they sat down, Mrs. Baldwin said, "I have behaved abominably to both of you. Will you accept my profoundest apologies?"

"Of course, we will," Jeremy said quickly.

Titania let his statement suffice, as she did not really feel in a forgiving mood.

"You have both been accommodating to me. I may not have thanked you, Titania, but there was many a time you saved my life, running all over town to find just the right pair of shoes or bag to go with a dress, luggage for my coat. I know I paid you well, but it was not enough compensation for my behavior in...well, with your husband before your eyes. It was unforgivable of me, but will you forgive me?"

Titania was suspicious. This was out of character for the lofty Karin Baldwin. What did she want? "It takes two to tango," said Titania, feeling something tacky was called for.

"Yes, it does take two." She smiled coldly. "And I realize I cannot put the blame for Acheson's betrayal entirely at your feet. In any case, I have decided not to oppose the opening of your store here in Naupaka. I have signed the waiver."

"Your kind understanding is overwhelming," said Titania, unimpressed, while Jeremy shot daggers at her. "I don't suppose this had anything to do with the receipt for clothes you purchased here, constituting proof of your approval?"

"How clever you are, my dear," said Mrs. Baldwin smiling. "But then, aside from your insistence on this affair with Acheson Lane, you've always impressed me with your intelligence." She stood up and her lawyer did the same. She seemed to have him on remote control.

"Karin." Jeremy placed an arm around her. "I know how you feel, but all this shouldn't affect our relationship."

Karin Baldwin give him an imperious gaze. "I will

never set foot across the threshold of Jeremy Evans, Ltd.
while she is your partner."

Titania's eyes suddenly lit up. It was a brilliant so-
lution to all their problems. Why hadn't she thought of
it before?

"All right," said Titania. "I don't hold anything
against Jeremy. We've always had a profitable, candid
business relationship, if not a very good marriage. And
you're too good a customer to lose. I have a proposal
you might find appealing."

She raised a haughty eyebrow. "Yes?"

"Why don't you buy me out? Become partners with
Jeremy."

"Why in the world should I do that?"

"Because there's no one on earth who knows and
enjoys good-looking clothes as much as you do, and
taking half interest in our store would probably amuse
you more than a dozen lovers."

To Jeremy's surprise, Mrs. Baldwin did not take of-
fense.

"I'd never considered that," she mused. Then she
looked suspiciously at Titania. "What is your price?"

"We can have our lawyers haggle over that," said
Titania, "the monetary price, that is."

"There is another price?" she asked.

"A few legal clauses, that's all." Titania smiled.

"What legal clauses?" Mrs. Baldwin's green eyes narrowed.

"To do with 'approval' of stores that can go into the
Naupaka and the decor—things like that."

"Oh, that." She laughed. "Naupaka was an amusing
project—but only when it had to do with Acheson Lane.
It's considerably less so now. A store in Beverly Hills
sounds much more appealing. All right, dear. You have

it. Well, come on, Jeremy," said Mrs. Baldwin with a pleased smile. "We have many things to discuss."

As soon as they left, Titania rushed out to the party to tell Acheson.

"If she's buying you out," he asked, "what are you going to do about your store here?"

"First, I'm going to change the sign outside. We'll take down the 'Jeremy Evans, Ltd.' and put up 'Titania's Sportswear.'"

He stopped the band from playing and raised his voice to make an announcement. "We have two things to celebrate today, and we are happy to have our guests and friends here to help us. You, of course, know the first, and that is the grand opening of this beautiful store, which will soon be changing its name. The second is the announcement of my marriage to Titania Evans."

There was wild applause as the band broke into a rendition of the "Hawaiian Wedding Song" while Acheson and Titania kissed.

Mama Vasco was the first to hug and congratulate them. "We'll have the wedding in the ranch house," she said. "I always think people should get married in a house."

"Mama Vasco," said Acheson, putting his arm around her, "we will have the reception there, but the wedding, no."

"But a hotel is no place for a wedding," she protested. "Yes, I know it is more elegant, perhaps, and it's *your* hotel, but...it's still a hotel."

"We don't want to be married in the hotel either," said Titania.

"You are going back to Los Angeles for the wedding? She could not mask her disappointment. "Well, maybe Henry will let us get tickets."

"No, no," said Acheson. "You will come to the wedding. The whole family will be there and then afterward we will have the reception at the ranch house."

"But if it's not at the hotel and not at my house, where are you going to have the wedding?"

"Menehune Caves," said Acheson and Titania at once, then laughed.

"But that's no place for a wedding."

"We promised the menehunes," said Titania firmly.

"Ah, come on, a smart businesswoman like you believing all that crazy stuff about the menehunes?" asked Mama Vasco playfully, her eyes twinkling.

Titania gazed at Acheson and smiled. "He made me a believer."

Second Chance at Love ™

Don't miss any of these breathless tales
of lovers lost and found! Order today!

FLAMENCO NIGHTS #1
by Susanna Collins
In the Cordoba of gold-hued days and soft, jasmine-scented
nights artist Rosie Powell risks heartbreak again when
she falls in love with world-famous flamenco guitarist—and
notorious womanizer—Juan de Arévalo.

WINTER LOVE SONG #2
by Meredith Kingston
Ski Champion Felicia Hollingsworth, still desperately in
love with her former coach and husband, Grant Mitchell,
meets him again on Sun Valley's seductive slopes. Can
she return to his life and not his arms—the place claimed
by another woman?

THE CHADBOURNE LUCK #3
by Lucia Curzon
The dazzling Lady Celia Chadbourne has a score to
settle with the darkly handsome Lord Armin Sherlay. But in
a risky play of hearts, passion becomes sweeter than
revenge...

OUT OF A DREAM #4
by Jennifer Rose
A dashing ad agency executive and a devastatingly handsome architect vie for Eileen Connor on a glamour assign-
ment in Switzerland.

GLITTER GIRL #5
by Jocelyn Day
Divorced, beautiful, Tiffany Harte returns to Cougar Beach
on the rugged Oregon coast and faces the scornful con-
tempt of her first real love, Clay.

Second Chance at Love ™

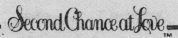
Second Chance at Love ™

WINDS OF MORNING #13
by Laurie Marath
Lovely Jennifer Logan believed she'd left troubled love far behind when she came to Glengarriff, the small village on Ireland's coast…until she met the most difficult, haunted—and completely wonderful—man in the world!

HARD TO HANDLE #14
by Susanna Collins
The Belgian aristocrat is a supremely talented equestrian and trainer, an arrestingly handsome, passionate man. But the moment beautiful, widowed Ariane Charles sees him, she knows he's more dangerous to her than an untamed stallion.

BELOVED PIRATE #15
by Margie Michaels
The crystal waters of the Bahamas hold the treasure-find of a lifetime…and the test of a lifetime, too, for stunning Lorelei Averill as she meets again the man she'd once loved too well.

PASSION'S FLIGHT #16
by Marilyn Mathieu
Cool and elusive as a spring mist, Beverly Milford resists the devastating charm of the celebrated lover who is her boss. In Paris, then Hawaii, her defenses erode and the lovely widow is in emotional peril…again.

HEART OF THE GLEN #17
by Lily Bradford
Roaming the byways of Scotland, scouting for antiques, Julie Boland encounters sharp-tongued Ian Fraser. His attractions are enormous, his emotions seem as fickle as her faithless ex-husband's… can the handsome laird erase Julie's bitter memories?

BIRD OF PARADISE #18
by Winter Ames
Brilliant as she is beautiful, Sara Mancini continues her agricultural experiments on Eric Thoreson's Panamanian coffee plantation—despite the interference of her late husband's family…of the tempestuous Rima…and of her irresistible employer.

**TO GET THESE BREATHLESS TALES
OF LOVERS LOST AND FOUND
PLEASE USE THE ORDER FORM
ON THE FOLLOWING PAGE**

Second Chance at Love ™

Jove's Thrilling New Romance Line

____	FLAMENCO NIGHTS #1 by Susanna Collins	05703-7
____	WINTER LOVE SONG #2 by Meredith Kingston	05637-5
____	THE CHADBOURNE LUCK #3 by Lucia Curzon	05624-3
____	OUT OF A DREAM #4 by Jennifer Rose	05777-0
____	GLITTER GIRL #5 by Jocelyn Day	05878-5
____	AN ARTFUL LADY #6 by Sabina Clark	05863-7
____	EMERALD BAY #7 by Winter Ames	05694-4
____	RAPTURE REGAINED #8 by Serena Alexander	05776-2
____	THE CAUTIOUS HEART #9 by Philippa Heywood	05801-7
____	ALOHA, YESTERDAY #10 by Meredith Kingston	05907-2
____	MOONFIRE MELODY #11 by Lily Bradford	05638-3
____	MEETING WITH THE PAST #12 by Caroline Halter	06132-8
____	WINDS OF MORNING #13 by Laurie Marath	05623-5
____	HARD TO HANDLE #14 by Susanna Collins	05704-5
____	BELOVED PIRATE #15 by Margie Michaels	06067-4
____	PASSION'S FLIGHT #16 by Marilyn Mathieu	05978-1
____	HEART OF THE GLEN #17 by Lily Bradford	05847-5
____	BIRD OF PARADISE #18 by Winter Ames	05977-3

All titles listed above are $1.75

Available at your local bookstore or return this form to:

 JOVE/BOOK MAILING SERVICE
P.O. Box 690, Rockville Center, N.Y. 11570

Please enclose 50¢ for postage and handling for one book, 25¢ each add'l. book ($1.50 max.). No cash, CODs or stamps. Total amount enclosed: $ _____ in check or money order.

NAME _____

ADDRESS _____

CITY _____ STATE/ZIP _____

Allow six weeks for delivery.   SK-25